Wreck and Ruin

By

Amy Corwin

Synopsis

*A mysterious wreck brings danger and romance to a
lonely heiress*

Society may not approve of a spinster establishing her
own home, but the *ton* hasn't meet Hannah. Her
audacious plans go awry, however, when her ship sinks off
the coast of Cornwall. She barely escapes wreckers, led by
a man wearing a griffin ring, only to find herself alone and
bereft of both her possessions and her reputation. When
Lord Blackwold and his grandmother grant her refuge,
she's still not safe. The attractive marquess is one of four
men wearing a griffin ring, any one of whom could be the
wrecker leader.

A strange accident, the specter of social ruin, and
Blackwold's annoying betrothal to another woman upset
Hannah's plans, but they can't stop her. Despite the
danger, she's determined to unmask the leader of the
wreckers and set her own course. Her trust in the
marquess may be foolish, but her heart insists that his love
is the key to finding her way home.

Copyright

This is a work of fiction. Names, characters, places, incidents either are the product of the author's imagination or are used fictitiously. Any resemblance to actual persons, living or dead, business establishments, events or locales, is entirely coincidental.

Wreck and Ruin

COPYRIGHT © 2017 by Amy G. Padgett

Contact information: contact@amycorwin.com
Editorial Services Provided by: Vince Dickinson
                                    Judy Lynn, *Judicious Revisions LLC*

Publishing History
First Edition, 2017
Second Edition, 2018

Table of Contents

Chapter One

February 18, 1828, Coast of Cornwall

The ship lurched beneath Hannah's feet, and the small box containing her jewelry flew out of her hands as her shoulder hit the wall of her cabin. Her mother's emerald and diamond necklace sparkled as it tumbled out of the box, random shafts of light catching the stones as the lantern swung wildly above her head.

She caught the edge of her bunk with cold fingers. The shriek of wooden timbers splintering against sharp-edged rocks broke through the maelstrom of howling wind and waves. Her stomach roiled sickeningly. Water slammed into the door of her cabin, rattling the flimsy barrier and rushing underneath to wash over the floor and saturate her delicate white satin slippers.

Already dressed for dinner—for her last dinner— aboard the *Orion* before it was to dock in Liverpool in the morning, she held on to a bedpost as the floor tilted beneath her feet. How could they wreck this close, go down just eighteen hours before she was due to reach England?

The ship bucked again, throwing off her question with a disdainful shrug and sending her falling onto her bed.

The necklace twined between her fingers as she clutched at the heavy coverlet, trying to regain her balance. Another wave pounded at her door and the ship tilted so sharply that, for a few seconds, the door slid into the floor's position.

We're going down! Without thinking, her hands scrabbled over the bed, snatching up her jewelry and tying it in her handkerchief. She stuffed it into a plain linen pocket, which she tied around her waist, not caring that it was over the thin white silk of her dress rather than properly hidden beneath her skirts. Her glance flew to the large, hump-backed chest in the corner. The swaying light

1

cast huge black shadows over the walls as her cabin shuddered. Timbers creaked and snapped as the vessel cracked against jagged rocks.

My papers—money! There was no time. Even as she threw herself at her trunk, the door burst open. Sea water flooded in. A world glimmering in gold and black swirled around her before the light was extinguished. An icy wave battered her against the wall and then pulled her out into the darkness, plunging her into the ocean.

Spars, a broken mast, and debris slammed into her as she kicked furiously, trying to get her mouth above the cold waves. Her eyes stung. All she could do was plunge under the swirling surface and kick furiously, trying to escape the pull of the sinking ship. Pushing upward, she gasped for air, freezing rain cutting against her cheeks and forehead.

A twinkle of light—a distant golden glow flickered amidst the swirling gray and black of the storm. Her heart leapt. Someone had seen the ship foundering against the rocky shoreline—someone had come to help! With strong strokes, she slipped through the crashing waves, blinking saltwater and rain out of her eyes as she fixed her gaze on that small yellow spark.

Something rough and yet yielding brushed her arm. A sodden, woolen coat. Another survivor? She grabbed at it, pulling it closer, only stare into the flat dead eyes of a sailor, the skin on the side of his face ripped and flapping loosely in the water, the flesh already drained of blood. Recognizing him with horror, she thrust him away and kicked toward the sharp, black teeth of the rocks guarding the shore.

Despite her efforts, the storm was reluctant to let Hannah escape so easily. Waves tumbled around her, teasingly drawing her away from the flickering light, only to toss her back against the rocks like an old, discarded doll. Her hands and arms stung from the salt and icy rain. The outcroppings were so sharp and so slippery with seaweed and water that she couldn't pull herself out, couldn't find a way to fight against the push and pull of the violent seas.

Part of a broken mast hit her back. She sucked in a mouthful of saltwater in a gasp of pain. Coughing and spitting out water, she grabbed hold of the spar, the wood smooth under her bruised hands. Sputtering, she kicked wearily—or thought she was kicking. Her limbs were so cold that she could no longer feel her feet.

Her body shook—her muscles no longer obeyed her—and the thought of giving up yanked at her. Was she even still holding on? She shifted her hands clumsily, locking her elbow over the bit of wood. A huge, black boulder loomed ahead of her.

No!

Thud! The tip of the mast hit the rock, jarring her. She tightened her grip and kicked wearily, wedging the spar between two massive stones. The toe of her right foot hit a small shelf beneath her, enough to stand tiptoe upon, but not high enough to give her purchase to scramble over the tumble of stones.

But it was enough to give her a moment to catch her breath.

"Any others?" a man's deep voice sliced through the gale.

She raised her head, her mouth open, but water rushed over her lips. She spit it out.

Yes—me! I'm here! The thought screamed through her.

In the fitful light, she could see broad shoulders draped in a heavy cloak. A wide-brimmed hat hid the man's face, and the fitful light made it impossible to see more than his general, slouching shape, but her hands tightened around the wood she clung to, hope flaring in her chest.

Rescuers! Someone had seen the ship—someone was trying to help them.

"An officer," another man replied before she could speak. "Clinging to a rock."

A sharp cry caught in Hannah's throat, the sound lost amidst the wailing of the wind and crashing of the waves. An officer! First Officer Edward Trent?

Her thoughts surged with hope. He'd been so kind to her during the month-long voyage from Boston, he'd even taken the time from his duties to bring her a cup of tea when she'd felt ill the first day out from port. And he'd survived—thank God! She wasn't the only one, there were others. There *had* to be!

"Push him off, then."

"But—"

"You have a club—use it."

What? The stark coldness and inhuman contempt in the man's words made Hannah's aching fingers stiffen. She tightened her arm around the broken mast, trying to stay afloat as her limbs shook uncontrollably.

Think! She must have misheard them—they couldn't possibly intend to murder a man as he struggled out of the punishing sea. Her mind whirled uselessly, terror making coherent thought as slippery as an eel.

All she could think about was Officer Trent's kind eyes. A surge of panic tore her breath away.

What about her companion, Mrs. Lawrence, and her maid? Surely, they were alive somewhere, had managed to make it to shore. These men wouldn't murder the helpless women, would they? The thought stalled in her mind, with the sickening certainty that if they used their clubs on Officer Trent, they were unlikely to leave anyone else alive.

Anyone.

Her mouth clamped shut as another wave washed over her face. She had to get out of the water soon, before she lost all strength and vitality. Her body was shaky and weak—she couldn't hold her precarious perch much longer.

An ugly chuckle greeted the closest man's remark, and the second man said, "The rock that caught him took care of him right and proper. Smashed his head in for us. No need to do nothing 'cept watch."

"Watch, then, and take care there are no other survivors. Her cargo is our only interest."

"Aye, sir."

A glint of light caught Hannah's attention. The man had placed his hand on the rock above her. A ring glinted in the false lights they'd set along the shore to trap the *Orion*. She stared at it. An animal face with dark eyes framed with wings. An animal as odious as the man wearing the ring.

I'll remember that—never forget it.

The hand disappeared, but the pounding of the waves, rain, and rocks around her obscured his departure.

And kept her safe from his notice.

Her heart hammered in her chest. She couldn't tell if he was standing amidst the rocks above her, or had moved further down the beach to search for the cargo washed to shore by the storm. If they'd murdered anyone else from the ship—her companion or other friends—she couldn't hear that, either.

She was grateful for that small mercy.

A strong undertow pulled at her feet and skirts, trying to yank her back into the ocean. The tension that had given her a small surge of hot energy faded beneath the cutting sheets of rain sluicing over her frozen cheeks.

She was risking her life to return to deeper water, but she couldn't stay where she was. The men might return and see her.

Struggling with the broken spar, she used the last of her strength to free it from the rocks. Then, fatalistically, she kicked weakly, trying to escape from what had felt like a safe, sheltered spot.

Much of the storm's fury had been spent, but the cold rain continued to beat down and the waves were no less treacherous. This time, Hannah steered away from the lights, away from the men on the rocky beach. She clung to the piece of wood and struggled against the current, knowing that the wreckers had positioned themselves to let the ocean carry the ship's treasures to them.

Exhausted and unable to kick her numb feet any more, she felt the waves crash her once more against the jagged shoreline. The spar hit the rocks with a jolt that sent pain arching through her shoulders and back. Darkness pressed all around her, and despite the sharply serrated surface of the boulder that had caught the spar, she pulled herself up and out of the water.

Warmth trickled down her wrists. Her saturated skirts caught on the rock, but she ruthlessly ripped them free and scrambled over the boulder to a small patch of sand between the large black stones.

She fell to her knees.

You can't stay here—it isn't safe, she told herself urgently. Her body shivered uncontrollably as rain beat down upon her head and shoulders. The fresh water washed away the burning salt, but did nothing to bring warmth back to her icy skin. Thankfully, the darkness was too complete to allow her to see much of her raw hands and ruined gown. Cold stones pressed against her knees, absorbing what little heat her limbs retained, but she closed her eyes for the moment, too weak and tired to care.

Unfortunately, her mind cared—too much—dredging up memories of Mrs. Lawrence, laughing at some wry, humorous tidbit, and Officer Trent, bending forward to offer a steaming cup of tea to her. She could almost feel the smoothness of the bone china cup and smell the scent of hot tea. Her thoughts spun in tight, frantic circles, on the edge of panic, trying to escape into the warm safety of memories instead of facing the stark reality of her situation.

The cove where the wreckers were busily scavenging couldn't be far, though the storm muffled the sound of their rough voices. The men would be searching for survivors, ready to club any who could still draw a breath. She had to escape from the beach and the restless sea.

Inland—it was the only way to safety.

But if she left the beach, wouldn't the villagers, anyone who lived nearby, be just as deadly? The men—the wreckers—had to live nearby. What would they do if a limping, bedraggled woman came to them for aid?

No survivors. They'd club her and throw her body back into the sea. Maintain their silence and their secrets.

Unable to help herself, she vomited, saltwater burning her mouth. One trembling hand went to the lumpy pocket she'd tied around her waist. Her jewelry was still there, for what that was worth. Bitterness whipped through her. Jewels were useless as a bribe. Why would anyone accept one bangle and leave her alive—and potentially dangerous to their interests—when they could murder her and have everything she owned? Her stomach heaved again, but she swallowed until the nausea passed.

First things first—all the jewelry in the world won't matter if I die here amidst these rocks.

She may have been born in Boston, but she was no sheltered Miss who'd seen nothing of the world except rose-covered wallpaper. Her father had cherished an unyielding, urgent need to travel, to see what lay beyond the next river or forest. And her mother refused to allow him to go alone, so she'd dragged their family with him, step by step, until accident, sickness, and then death had claimed Hannah's brothers and sisters, her mother, and finally, her father.

Everyone except Hannah. She'd survived the loss of her family, and she'd survive this. And maybe then she'd finally find the one thing she'd longed for through all the hardships and pain of loss: a home of her own in the country of her father's youth. England.

Even if that country seemed ready to kill her the moment she set foot on its rocky, inhospitable shore.

No matter. She'd get away from the beach and she'd survive, no matter what foul deeds the men on the beach did. She'd live and go to London as she planned, and become the toast of the town. And she'd find her own home.

Hannah fixed her gaze on the jagged darkness of the rocks rising in a cliff towering over the shore. There was a path there—there had to be. And she would find it before the men could find her.

Chapter Two

A carriage! Hannah stood in the center of the silvery-gray ribbon of road and waved her arms, praying the driver could see her, despite the misty rain. Behind her, she heard booted feet scrabbling up the cliff. If they saw her...

She shivered, feeling exposed at the top of the cliffs. The storm's rage had lessened, and she caught the occasional voice and scrape of leather soles from the scavengers below.

"Any others?" A man's voice echoed faintly through the growing mist.

She stumbled along the road in the direction of the carriage, gesturing more frantically.

The clatter of horses and creaking of a heavy carriage rattled above the other noises. Hannah glanced over her shoulder.

If the men on the beach heard... Were they already climbing up to the road?

The vehicle rumbled closer. She waved her arms again, stepping toward the ditch edging the road. The coach had to stop! She cast another glance at the cliff. Something dark bobbed in the darkness, barely visible. Panic tightened in her chest.

"Whoa!" At the last minute, the coachman pulled back on the reins. The four horses snorted and threw their heads up, gray puffs of warm air ringing their mouths as they stamped past her.

Hannah stumbled into the ditch and dragged herself upright as the coach rolled several yards beyond her before stopping. Lunging for the door, her hands slapped the side panel as she fell against the vehicle.

She didn't dare look over her shoulder to see what was happening at the top of the cliff, a few hundred yards away.

"Beamish! Why are we stopping?" An imperious female voice called from inside the carriage.

"A figure on the road—the Lady of the Mist!" the coachman replied, his voice shaking.

"Lady of the Mist! Pshaw! None of that spirit nonsense—the vicar won't stand for it if he hears you." The occupant of the carriage thumped against the side of the carriage. "Carry on—we shall never reach Blackrock if you insist on stopping for every bit of mist."

"Stop—please!" Hannah called, pounding the panel and grabbing at the handle of the door again.

"Who is that?" the coach occupant asked sharply. "Step away from my carriage immediately! Beamish—drive on! Now!"

Wrenching the door open, Hannah flung herself inside, her shoulder banging painfully against the floor. "Please— the ship—wrecked!" she gasped.

"Who are you? Remove yourself immediately! Beamish!"

Hannah reached out and caught at the stout figure swathed in blankets on the seat next to her. "Please, you must help me. I was a passenger on the *Orion*. We sank!"

The carriage jolted and shook as the coachman climbed down, mumbling under his breath.

"*Please!*" Hannah begged, searching the shadows for the face of the woman next to her. "In God's name— please!"

"Who are you?" the woman asked. She was so bundled up with a large bonnet, shawls, and blankets that Hannah could barely make out the short, round shape in the darkness.

A light streamed over Hannah's shoulder as she pulled herself up to her knees inside the coach. The golden glow flickered over the occupant's face, revealing broad cheekbones under heavily wrinkled, sagging skin, and eyes shadowed under shaggy gray brows.

"I am Hannah Cowles—Miss Hannah Cowles, from Boston."

The elderly lady shifted beneath her blankets and chuckled. "Well, Miss Hannah Cowles from Boston, it may have escaped your notice, but this is a private vehicle. You are intruding." She sniffed. "And we have not been properly introduced. I am not in the habit of picking up strange women on the road. Now, if you will do me the kindness of descending from my carriage, we shall be on our way." She gazed at Hannah with a bland expression, although, despite the shadowy interior of the carriage, Hannah could have sworn the elderly lady's eyes held a mischievous light.

"No." Hannah's chin rose. "I insist you take me to the nearest..." She paused in consternation. Where exactly could she go? She had nothing... She shivered and rubbed her wet arms, wincing as seawater burned her hands.

All her clothing was in her luggage—her *luggage*! Her letters of introduction and more importantly, the letter to the bank, were inside her trunk. Without those documents, she truly had nothing and no way to prove who she was. Instead of arriving triumphantly in London as a rich American heiress, she was arriving destitute—completely ruined. A flutter of panic chilled her. She rubbed her arms faster.

"You are bleeding upon my upholstery, Miss Cowles." The old lady sighed elaborately. "And I just had everything redone. What a nuisance."

Hannah glanced down and sighed. A long gash on her right leg bled sluggishly, staining her white gown. Her sleeves were tattered, revealing cuts and abrasions on her arms and the palms of her hands.

All of that paled in comparison to her dress. Her best evening gown—her only gown at this point—was ruined.

She'd wanted to look her best for their last supper on the *Orion*, so she'd had Lizzy take out her white satin with its pale pink gauze overdress and bodice sewn with pearls and white silk roses. Oddly enough, her pearl earrings, necklace, and bracelet had survived her ordeal and felt warm against her chilled skin.

But her skirts were torn and smeared with mud. Only one white satin slipper remained, freezing into a sodden mess on her left foot. A long strand of blackish seaweed hung off one of the pearls in the center of her neckline. She plucked it off and, after a moment's hesitation, flung it out of the door over the coachman's bulky shoulder.

"I do apologize," Hannah replied coolly. "It is a nuisance, indeed."

"Lady Blackwold?" Beamish asked, holding his lantern up to peer at the elderly lady. He glanced from her to Hannah and back, clearly reluctant to drag Hannah out of the carriage by force.

A distant yell caught her attention. Hannah stared into the darkness beyond the coachman's shoulder. The wreckers—that black shape rising above the edge of the cliff—she'd forgotten them. If they discovered her now, they'd know she'd escaped them.

She opened her mouth to warn the coachman about the men on the beach and to beg them to move on. She glanced at Lady Blackwold. The older woman was watching her, wearing a strange grin, as if she were well aware of Hannah's predicament and found it amusing.

A stab of mistrust made Hannah snap her mouth shut. The storm was sufficient to explain what had happened to the *Orion* and her own condition. No need to mention the wreckers or what she'd seen.

Maybe they'd let her live if they thought she hadn't seen anything.

Lady Blackwold's smile widened. She shifted, poking around on the seat beside her. Finally, she picked up a gray bundle and tossed it to Hannah. "I dislike sacrificing a perfectly good woolen blanket, but your lips are blue, and I like that even less."

"Oh dear, blue lips are *très chic* in Boston. I felt sure they would inspire a new fashion when I arrived in London." Hannah shook out the blanket and wrapped it gratefully around her shoulders.

"Lady Blackwold?" Beamish asked again from the door, his gruff voice rising as his confusion increased.

"Oh, do be quiet, Beamish," Lady Blackwold said. "And close that blasted door. You are allowing that filthy night air into the coach, and you know how unhealthy that is."

He stared at her, his mouth sagging open. "Lady Blackwold?"

"Drive on, you fool! Drive on to Blackrock!" Lady Blackwold unearthed a cane from her bundle of blankets and pushed the tip into the center of his chest, forcing him away from the door.

"Lady Blackwold!" Beamish gaped, the lantern swinging wildly in his gloved hand as he tried to maintain his balance by grabbing the door with his other hand.

"Go on and be quick about it!"

"Yes, Lady Blackwold!" Beamish regained his footing and slammed the door shut, though Hannah could hear him mumbling an assortment of rich curses that proved the coachman's dull appearance belied his vast and impressive knowledge of the English language.

The carriage jerked and dipped down as Beamish climbed into his perch, and with another wrenching jolt, it surged forward. The clatter of horse hooves made it impossible to hear if anyone shouted from the cliffs.

"Well, Miss Cowles, I cannot comprehend how you came to be wandering the roads at night, dressed like that," Lady Blackwold said, clearly determined to catch Hannah out in a lie.

Hannah smiled blandly. "I wanted to look my best for my last evening aboard the *Orion*. We were to dock in Liverpool tomorrow morning, but the storm blew us off course. The ship wrecked—I was lucky to escape alive."

"You are the only survivor?"

"I sincerely hope not," Hannah replied, thinking again about Officer Trent's kind smile. Sadness pulled at her, and she tightened the blanket around her shoulders as another sick tremor wracked her. She swallowed several times, her lips pressed together.

What of her companion and maid?

Poor Lizzy hadn't wanted to come—she was afraid of the water and couldn't swim—but Hannah had only joked about her maid's fears as they boarded the *Orion* in Boston. Now, she wondered if Lizzy had had some notion of what was to befall the packet, barely eighteen hours before they were to dock.

"Did you see anyone else?" Lady Blackwold persisted, her round wrinkled face hidden in the deep shadows beneath her large black bonnet.

Hannah shook her head. "I managed to cling to a piece of wood and barely made it to shore. It was all I could do to climb up to the road. I hoped to find a village—assistance."

"Is there any point in notifying the authorities? A Custom Officer, perhaps?"

"Oh, yes, the authorities must be informed," Hannah said, trying not to shiver. "There may be others—and my trunk. I must have my trunk." Her fortune depended upon the documents in her trunk.

Despite the scratchy folds of the heavy woolen blanket, she still felt frozen. Her body shook uncontrollably, and although she was wary, she had difficulties concentrating. Her eyes fluttered shut for a moment. She sat up with a jerk and blinked furiously.

The wheezy sound of Lady Blackwold's muffled laughter aroused a brief, hot flash of anger in Hannah.

"You amuse me, Miss Cowles. You may be, as I suspect, an adventuress setting out to fleece an elderly lady who should know better, but at least you are no mealy-mouthed sycophant."

"I am *not* an adventuress!"

"Of course not," Lady Blackwold agreed with another laugh.

"I am an heiress—I booked first class passage on the *Orion*."

"Of course. It is unfortunate, though, that unless I miss my guess, you can prove none of this?"

"I—my trunk..." Hannah sputtered to a halt.

"Naturally. The missing trunk. So very convenient," Lady Blackwold murmured.

"It is not at all convenient! I've lost everything—all my letters of introduction, the letters to the bank and my London lawyer—*everything*!"

Lady Blackwold's large bonnet dipped as she nodded.

"I could hardly have known that your carriage would be passing by at that particular moment. It would have been the height of foolishness to plan on such a thing. I could have *died* of exposure in the rain before anyone came. I may be an American, but I'm not that much of a fool."

"No. Anyone could see that," Lady Blackwold agreed dryly.

Hannah bit the inside of her cheek to avoid the sarcastic reply hovering in her mouth.

"What are your plans now, Miss Cowles?"

"Now? Why I—" Her grip on the blanket tightened. She slipped her left hand over her hip and felt the lumpy pocket still tied at her waist.

She was not without resources, but that was truly a double-edged sword. If she sold her jewels, she'd have funds, at least until they ran out. And then what? The very presence of the jewelry gave some credence to her claim to be an heiress. Without them, she was just a woman making unsubstantiated statements.

And the diamond and emerald necklace had been her mother's. Could she really sell that?

"Yes?"

"I don't know. I haven't had time to consider what I should do. If I could find my trunk and my papers, I could travel on to London as I'd planned. There is a lawyer there who expects me, and funds have been transferred to a bank—"

"But you have no papers, my dear. Have you met this lawyer?"

Hannah shook her head and blinked rapidly. She was so cold and tired—she couldn't think anymore, didn't want to consider the difficulties ahead of her. She just wanted to close her eyes and let go. Sleep.

Another chill shook her and her grip on the blanket tightened to keep it from slipping off her shoulders.

"Have you been introduced to anyone in London? Anyone in England?"

"No." Hannah jerked upright.

"Pity."

"If I could find my trunk—"

"Of course. Well, I am sure if it exists, it may float to shore with all the other flotsam and jetsam."

Hannah nodded, too tired to parry Lady Blackwold's verbal thrust.

"I have found it very boring of late," Lady Blackwold commented when Hannah remained silent. "It would amuse me if you would be my guest." She chuckled. "At least until this mysterious trunk is found."

"Thank you." Her shoulders drooped in relief.

"I have a great dislike of gratitude, so if you experience that emotion, I hope you will have the good sense to keep it to yourself."

"Yes, Lady Blackwold."

"And meekness. I was never given to understand that American girls suffered greatly from meekness. Was I mistaken?"

"No, Lady Blackwold." Hannah tried to invest as much spirit as possible in her reply.

"I hope I will not be given cause to regret my generosity."

"I suppose that will depend on just how generous you intend to be."

Lady Blackwold's chuckles turned into a cough, but she waved Hannah back when she leaned forward in concern. "I don't know if I have any faith in this trunk of yours, but perhaps you will be fortunate and there will be a long delay in finding it."

"Yes," Hannah replied dryly. "That would be fortunate, wouldn't it?"

With that, Hannah leaned back, shut her eyes, and pretended to fall asleep.

Chapter Three

The carriage jerked to a halt in front of a rambling house that rose in the darkness like an extension of the cliffs themselves. Hannah, shaking with a chill, glanced out of the window as Beamish assisted Lady Blackwold to descend. The cold had sunk its teeth so deeply into the marrow of her bones that Hannah felt she'd never be warm again. Her damp gown clung to her limbs, and the salty water had soaked into the blanket she'd wrapped around her shoulders, so even the heavy folds failed to hold back the penetrating February cold.

Trembling violently, she had to accept Beamish's arm around her waist to assist her to alight and help her up the broad stone steps. Lady Blackwold had apparently given a great many orders concerning her guest, for Hannah no sooner set foot in the front hall than a stern-faced maid took charge of her and led her to a door just beyond the grand staircase. She was whisked into a small room near the kitchen, stripped, and thrust into a tin bath, which another maid was hurriedly filling with buckets of steaming water.

The stern-faced maid chafed Hannah's hands and arms before dipping a coarse sponge into the steaming water and rubbing Hannah's back. A prickling sensation rushed over her numb skin and gradually, the blue tinge faded to pink and then to the deep red of a boiled lobster.

"I be Mary, Miss," the dour maid said as she dumped another bucket of near-boiling water over Hannah's head.

Before Hannah could answer, Mary hauled her out of the tub, rubbed her down as if she were a sweaty horse, and bundled her into a huge flannel nightgown, robe, and slippers. With frightening efficiency, she wrapped gauze around the palms of Hannah's hands and over the gash on her shin.

"Now off to bed with you, and I'll have a tray of some of Mrs. Mundy's veal broth—not that she'll be pleased about it, this time of night—brought to you." She wrapped an arm around Hannah and marched her back down the hallway to the grand staircase, up the stairs, and into a bedroom before she could say a word.

"Thank you," Hannah managed to mumble as Mary tucked her into the bed and fluffed the pillows behind her. A huge yawn cracked her jaw. As she settled under the heavy warmth of the feather-filled covers, she could barely keep her eyes open.

The terrors of the storm, her plunge into the ocean, and dangerous climb up the cliffs had left her battered and so exhausted that she could barely remain awake long enough to eat the pale soup Mary fed to her or drink the steaming cup of tea. But at last, the maid picked up the tray, blew out the candles, and left her in peace.

"Good morning, Miss," Mary said, startling Hannah out of a deep dreamless sleep. She thrust open the blue drapes to let a strong beam of wintry sunlight slap Hannah in the face.

Hannah blinked and held up a hand, surprised for a moment to see the thick bandage around her palms. The dreadful events of the previous night came rushing back as she turned her head away from the brilliant light.

"What time is it?" Hannah asked, glancing around the room for a clock.

She hadn't noticed—or cared—about her surroundings last night, but this morning, she was pleasantly surprised. The bedroom was large, with two chairs and a low table forming a gracious sitting area in front of a fireplace with a lovely delicately carved white mantle. The walls were papered with a pale blue and white Grecian print and darker blue curtains framed a wide window. A swan-legged desk and chair stood near the window to take advantage of the sunlight for writing letters. A silver inkstand and pen holder sat on top, gleaming in the light, and a collection of quill pens, all ready for her use, sat in a milk glass vase. A huge wardrobe took up most of the space along the wall next to the door, and a chest rested on the floor at the foot of the bed.

It was a room designed to wrap the occupant in soothing, pale blue comfort.

"Eleven, Miss. The dowager figured as you'd rested enough. She be anxious for you to join her at her supper. She eats at noon, you see. Always has."

Hannah threw back the covers and then paused, staring at Mary's plain, dour face in consternation. "My gown?"

"I'll do my best to mend it, but it'll never look the same." She lifted her arm, which had several articles of clothing draped over it. "I've worked over several of the dowager's gowns—she were quite the article of fashion in her time—and I've trunks more if you decide they suit you." Mary draped the items over the chest and selected one gown, a cerulean blue morning dress of jaconet muslin, and held it up, along with a darker blue Spencer.

The waistline of the dress was slightly higher than the current fashion, as was the short Spencer, and she eyed them with some misgivings. But although she knew it wasn't quite the thing to wear a Spencer indoors, it would grant her some much needed warmth, and she ought to be grateful, as she had nothing else to wear.

Unfortunately, the short jacket would emphasize the too-high waistline of the old-fashioned dress, but that couldn't be helped. With her bare feet dangling over the edge of the bed, she was all too aware of the drafts in the room that even the cheerful fire crackling in the fireplace couldn't vanquish.

"That gown looks lovely, Mary. I can't begin to thank Lady Blackwold for her generosity. And you for altering those gowns for me." Hannah walked quickly over to the small washstand, wriggling her toes against the icy currents of air. She quickly washed her face, trying not to notice the knotted mess of her hair, hanging down her back.

"In her day, the dowager were dark. You be so fair the colors aren't the best." Mary shrugged and waited as Hannah dried her face. "I brung you a shawl—in case you suffer from the cold." She sniffed, clearly believing that a true lady of quality would never deign to allow a mere draft to affect her.

"The cerulean is beautiful." At least the color would reflect the darker blue of her eyes. "Does the dowager live here alone?"

Hannah glanced over her shoulder to see Mary's lips tighten into a thin line.

So, there were limits to the kinds of questions she was willing to answer about her employer. Not that one was supposed to gossip with servants, anyway. Living in Boston had taught Hannah that much.

However, the maid's reaction made Hannah wonder why she was so reluctant to answer the simple question of who else lived at Blackrock.

"Never mind," Hannah said with a light laugh. "I'm sure I will meet whomever Lady Blackwold feels is appropriate."

"There be no doubt of that, Miss," Mary replied, holding a handful of stockings and undergarments, ready to assist Hannah to dress. The maid clearly underestimated Hannah's curious and open nature, however.

"Is it very cold this morning? The sunshine looks so warm," Hannah said.

Mary might not want to be amiable, but Hannah enjoyed making friends and was already prepared for the English desire to discuss the weather *ad nauseum*. She could talk about clouds, cirrus and cumulus, wind, and the possibility of precipitation until she cracked through the hardest shell.

Shrugging, Mary helped Hannah slip the blue gown over her head. "February always be cool."

"Cool? I should say this is quite cold for this area, is it not? I had always heard that southern England has warm winters."

"Cornwall?" Mary corrected her. "It be warm enough for any body, as I reckon it. Shall I brush your hair?"

Hannah grimaced. "If you can. It is so full of knots that I don't know if it will ever be possible to get a brush through the tangles."

"Never fear." For the first time that morning, a slight smile turned up the corners of Mary's thin lips. "I've brung the dowager's French pomatum. It'll do the trick, and it be made of lard—not nasty bear grease, as some use." She pulled a small, blue jar out of the pocket of her apron and opened it, holding it out for Hannah to see. "Made it myself."

The fragrant scents of lavender, orange flowers, and jasmine filled the cool air, and Hannah grinned with delight. "That smells lovely—thank you so much for thinking of it. It was very kind of you."

Blushing, Mary stared at the floor and mumbled under her breath as she guided Hannah to a ladder-backed chair near the washstand. She dipped her work-worn fingers into the pomade, rubbed it between her palms and began working it through Hannah's hair. The scent was so soothing and delightful that Hannah closed her eyes and breathed deeply. Before she knew it, her hair was free of tangles and twisted into a sophisticated knot at the base of her neck.

"There," Mary announced, stepping back.

Startled, Hannah stood and moved to stand in front of the mirror. Her hair almost glowed golden-blonde in the sunshine, smooth and fragrant.

"The dowager'll be waiting," Mary reminded her, putting the blue jar back into her apron pocket and stepping to the door. "I'll show you the way."

"Thank you, Mary."

Staring at the floor, Mary murmured a vague reply.

Hannah followed her, repressing a sigh. She might not have been able to win over the dour maid yet, but with luck, there was still time, and she had the inescapable feeling that she was going to need friends.

Nonetheless, despite her determination, a sigh escaped her as she followed the maid down the grand staircase.

One night's rest had not completely restored her, and her limbs felt stiff and achy. The gashes on her palms and shin throbbed and itched under their gauze wrappings, and a permanent chill had settled into her muscles.

She was still staring thoughtfully at the maid's thin, rigid back when Mary stopped at a wide doorway and stood aside.

"Miss Cowles, Lady Blackwold," Mary announced. She curtsied and waited, eyes downcast, for Hannah to enter.

The dowager, seated at the head of a long cherry table, was resplendent in a brilliant red silk dress, with thick ruffles of lace frothing at the neckline and wrists. An astounding confection constructed from the same red silk and lace, with the addition of several curly white feathers, covered her thick gray hair.

She nodded to Hannah and waved at the chair on her left. An elegant place setting of delicate, gilt-edged china and beautifully polished silver awaited her, and Hannah noticed that there were two other place settings on the dowager's right.

"Good morning, Lady Blackwold. How are you?" Hannah's hand touched the base of her neck. Her fingertips brushed her bare skin, missing the smooth warmth of her pearls.

My pearls! Where are my pearls! And the pocket containing her family jewelry? They'd taken her dress and belongings while she'd bathed, after her arrival. What had they done with them?

The dowager grinned at her and held up her right hand. "It occurred to me that you might be concerned about the whereabouts of these." The stained bag containing Hannah's jewels rested in the dowager's palm. "They are very impressive. Assuming they are real."

"Of course, they are real!" Hannah said, striding over to the chair at the dowager's left. She forced herself to adopt a calm, cheerful smile. "So, I am understandably relieved to see that I didn't lose them. Thank you."

"Did you imagine we would steal them?"

"No, of course not."

"Sit, then." The dowager motioned impatiently to the chair next to her. "My eyesight is not as good as it once was, so it was difficult to be sure if those jewels were paste or not. Though the pearls appeared valuable enough in the dim glow of the carriage lamp."

"Well, they are exactly what they appear to be." Hannah accepted the small bundle and after a moment's hesitation, placed it on the table to the left of her place setting before she took her seat. "I must thank you again for ensuring their safety." She resolutely refused to open the bag to check the contents in front of the dowager.

The dowager picked up her napkin and shook it out just as footsteps clattered across the floor. Both women glanced up, and the dowager's grin widened.

"Blackwold! So, you decided to join us after all," the dowager said, her dark eyes brightening.

A huge, shambling bear of a man, with shaggy brown hair and wide shoulders, ambled over to the dowager. He kissed her cheek before throwing himself into the chair on her right. His neckcloth was awry, and his dark blue jacket had clearly seen better days, as the elbows were worn, and the cuffs barely covered his strong wrists.

Hannah judged him to be in his mid to late twenties, and her first impression was that he was quite handsome, with a determined, square chin, wide Nordic cheekbones, and a proud nose. But his expression was so abstracted and distant that she immediately revised her opinion. Most likely, he was one of those peers her father had commented on with such disgust; one in whom intelligence had long ago been bred out of the deteriorating line to leave only a sort of doddering, drooling wreck of a human being.

"Blackwold! Adam!" the dowager repeated with increasing exasperation, her hands curling into small fists that she banged on the edge of the table. "Pay attention! We have a guest!"

His brow wrinkled. "Grandmother?"

23

"Yes—honestly, Blackwold. What is it that concerns you now and prevents you from noticing anything except your plate?"

"Now?" He gazed at her. "Dinner, I would think." He picked up his napkin and flung it into his lap, his brows rising as he looked at the dowager. "What else would I have on my plate?"

"Truly, you do this deliberately to annoy me—I am quite sure of it," the dowager said, frowning.

A grin widened his mouth, and he jerked his head back to fling a thick lock of hair out of his brown eyes. "I shouldn't think so. But good food deserves deliberation, and you always set an excellent table, Grandmother. You must forgive me if it distracted me."

"I was not talking about eating."

He glanced at her again, his brows rising.

"You know perfectly well I was not. Where are your manners? Must you act like such an *oaf* when we have guests?"

"Guests?" He glanced around, his brown eyes resting only momentarily upon Hannah.

For half a second, she thought she saw a flicker of deep, amused intelligence in his glance, and she held her breath, suddenly feeling confused. A heated flush rose to her cheeks, and she dropped her gaze to the table. Her hands fluttered over her plate, and she picked up her napkin and shook it out, almost flinging it over her shoulder in her nervousness. Her flaming cheeks grew hotter.

Blackwold grinned again. "I thought you said it was only a bit of flotsam that you found last night. Or jetsam—I always confuse those. A bit of something washed up on the beach, at any event." He looked at his grandmother. "Speaking of which, we had another wreck last night, poor devils. Blown off course." Another wide smile stretched his mouth. "It's hardly surprising to find flotsam and jetsam everywhere."

"Miss Cowles, may I present my grandson, Lord Blackwold?" the dowager said in the dry voice of extreme

24

exasperation. "Blackwold, Miss Hannah Cowles. Of Boston."

"Just that little bit of flotsam," Hannah murmured before fixing a smile on her face and nodding. "I am pleased to make your acquaintance, Lord Blackwold."

Blackwold's chair squealed in protest as he pushed it back to sketch a brief bow before he sat down again. "Pleasure's all mine, Miss Cowles."

"Miss Cowles was apparently a passenger on that ship, Blackwold," the dowager said as she gestured to a gangly red-haired footman to begin serving dinner.

"Indeed, I was. The *Orion*," Hannah added as the footman ladled white veal soup into the dish in front of her.

As if there were truly any doubt that I was a passenger. Apparently, indeed, she thought, studying her bowl. The delicious meaty, slightly salty fragrance reminded her of the warming broth she'd eaten the night before. Clearly, it formed the base of the soup today.

"I understood there were no survivors," Blackwold commented as he picked up a spoon and began eating.

Hannah's heart thudded, and she caught her breath. *No survivors.* Her spoon clattered against the side of the bowl.

No one else had made it to shore and escaped the men waiting for them on the beach.

Hot tears pricked her eyes. She blinked rapidly, concentrating on slowly eating her soup. Her grief was so intense, so overwhelming that she could barely swallow. She'd had dear friends on board the *Orion*—all those pleasant souls looking forward to one last supper together before docking—all of them, gone.

She'd hoped—truly prayed—that someone else might have survived.

She took a deep breath and gritted her teeth against another deep surge of emotion. Not wanting the others to see how badly the tragedy affected her, she forced herself to continue eating a few more spoonfuls. The slightest hint of mace was soothing and familiar, reminding her of being tucked under the thick blankets the previous evening, but the sensation did nothing to assuage her feelings of loss and loneliness. She put her spoon down.

"Miss Cowles apparently survived and managed to climb to the road, where she forced Beamish to halt the carriage." The dowager finished her soup and waved to a maid.

The girl hurried to join the footman and clear away the bowls. With her help, the footman began serving the roasted duck, poached eels, large rack of beef, and several dishes of vegetables that formed the second course.

"Brave, indeed." Blackwold chuckled. "And resourceful. I am not sure I'd trust old Beamish to halt on that road. Not at night."

Another hot flush burned Hannah's cheeks, embarrassed for no real reason. She kept her eyes on her plate and pushed a small piece of fish from one side of her plate to the other. "It was not particularly brave. I had no choice."

Blackwold's gaze flashed to his grandmother. She grinned, and in that small, silent communication, Hannah had a sense of the loving bond that existed between the two. And more than that, she realized something important about the dowager's character. Lady Blackwold was one of those who adored verbal duels—matching wits with an opponent. Her words were often insulting—even cruel—not with mean spirits, but because she hoped to provoke a rapier-sharp response.

Unfortunately, Hannah's blade was usually so rusted in its scabbard that she couldn't respond in time, and sadly, she was better known for her honesty than her wit.

When she glanced up, Blackwold's gaze was resting on the lumpy bag on the table next to Hannah's plate.

"Odd way to carry around jewelry—one would think," he said thoughtfully. "Surprised you retained the forethought to take it if the ship was sinking."

"I was dressing for dinner!" Hannah stared at him, but he was busy spearing a bit of cauliflower. She glanced at Lady Blackwold.

Lady Blackwold chuckled and shrugged, stepping aside from this particular duel.

"You saw—I was wearing my best gown!" Hannah added.

"You *were* dressed inappropriately for the weather," the dowager admitted. "As I noted before."

"I was in my evening gown—dressing for dinner—when the ship hit the rocks! And I had my jewelry out to decide what to wear. I..." Her chin rose. "I just put them into the pocket without thinking."

"Took them without thinking," Blackwold commented absently, his attention seemingly focused on reducing the mound of vegetables on his plate.

"I did *not* take them! They are mine!" Hannah's voice rose. "The emerald and diamond necklace belonged to my mother; my father gave it to her when they were married! Before I was born!"

"I am sure he did," Lady Blackwold said. "No need to weep about it."

"I am not crying," Hannah said, wiping the back of her hand over her damp cheeks. She felt beleaguered and almost feverish with desperation, despite her insight in the dowager's difficult character.

What were they accusing her of? Stealing? All she wanted to do was to go back upstairs, crawl into bed, and stay there. Her back ached where she'd been hit, and her hands were growing stiff under the light gauze covering her palms.

"What brought you to England, Miss Cowles?" Blackwold asked, changing the subject abruptly.

Hannah swallowed and took a deep breath. "I wanted to see London; my father spoke about it." She was *not* going to admit that she'd hoped to join Polite Society and enjoy a Season as a wealthy American heiress before purchasing her own estate—her own home.

Her dream seemed further away than ever, however. Her trunk—everything she'd possessed—was gone.

"Your father?" Blackwold glanced at her, the sharp sparkle of probing intelligence in his dark brown eyes.

"Lord Rothguard," Hannah replied proudly, staring at him in challenge.

Lady Blackwold laughed and shook her head. "Ah, I see. *That* Cowles." She wiped her lips with her napkin. "That barony is dormant, my dear. The last in the line, Richard Cowles, never claimed the title—went off to the colonies or some such nonsense—or so I heard. In any event, if you are the sole living child of that line, I suspect the title will go extinct. There is no Lord Rothguard—hasn't been since I was a girl." She smiled at Hannah. "I have a Debrett's if you wish to see it."

Hannah studied her, disconcerted. So, her father wasn't a baron. He was still the son of a baron, so how could it really matter?

"*Debrett's Peerage and Baronetage*," the dowager clarified.

"Well, titles are not used in Boston. It does not matter," Hannah said, staring down at a small piece of eel rapidly cooling on her plate. The strong, oily odor, originally so appetizing, made her stomach churn. "The only point I was trying to make was that the jewels are mine. I inherited them from my father. And mother."

"Or managed to slip them into your pocket before the ship foundered." Lady Blackwold waved her hand as if shooing away any protest Hannah might make. "No matter. You are here now. It will be amusing to see what Society makes of you when we remove to London next week."

Blackwold pushed his plate away and rose to his feet. "Excuse me, Grandmother. Miss Cowles." Without waiting for a reply, he strode out.

Watching his stiff shoulders as he left, Hannah had the distinct impression that he was annoyed.

His grandmother must have noticed it, as well, for she chuckled and waved to the red-haired footman to remove her empty plate. "My grandson is not looking forward to the Season, I fear. But he must go and at least pretend to have some affection for Lady Alice. It is time for him to attend a few dances at Almack's with her and show that he can be a gentleman, when he wishes."

Hannah caught her gaze, and the dowager shook her head.

"He is a marquess, you see, and Lady Alice is the daughter of an earl." Her dark eyes glittered. "After all, he must look far higher than the supposed daughter of a man who could not be bothered to claim his title. No, indeed. He shall marry Lady Alice or one of the girls vetted and approved by the patronesses of Almack's. The Marriage Mart does have its uses, you see."

"To keep wealthy American heiresses from marrying peers, perhaps?" Hannah replied coolly.

"To keep peers from making social blunders by marrying those who are inappropriate," the dowager corrected her complacently. She leaned forward, her small fists supporting her against the edge of the table. "I hope we haven't disappointed you, Miss Cowles, by explaining our circumstances. We may seem rude, or even cruel, but you must realize; you could be anyone. My grandson has not confided in you, but I have been known..." She shrugged and sat back. Sighing, she said, "Other supposed ladies before you have tried to take advantage of me." Her mouth twisted, and her fingers moved restlessly as she picked up and twisted her napkin. "I dislike speaking of it, but it is best that you understand the situation. I must live here with my grandson because I have no real choice. I was once quite as wealthy as you may have hoped. Well, there is no point in tiring you with boring memories. Suffice it to say, you will not find your fortune here." Her sharp gaze softened. "And you must not take what any of us say to heart. We are all known for little thought and sharp tongues. I only meant to warn you that if you are an adventuress taking advantage of the wreck of the *Orion* to assume a position not your own, you would be well advised to admit it now. I will not hold it against you, my dear."

"I am *not* an adventuress. I am Hannah Cowles, daughter of Richard Cowles, son of Lord Rothguard."

Lady Blackwold nodded wearily and rubbed her napkin over her mouth again. "You might regret surviving the *Orion*, then, for I imagine your reputation is quite ruined after last night."

"Simply because I was silly enough to survive?"

"Because you were wandering alone, at night, in the company of disreputable men." She lifted her brows. "Did you think we did not see the men climbing up to the road behind you?"

"I—" Hannah felt shaken at the thought that the wreckers had been that close to her—close enough to be seen by the dowager.

Lady Blackwold held up a gnarled hand. "Young ladies do not wander the roads of England alone. Particularly at night. And apparently, no one can identify you or perform introductions on your behalf. Other than me, of course."

"But I—my trunk! If someone finds my trunk, I have documents—letters of introduction. If we could find my trunk..."

"Who is to say that you are Hannah Cowles and not her maid? Or this companion you spoke of? 'Tis a pity you thought to save your jewelry instead of those documents."

Hannah stared at her. "If the trunk is found, I'm sure I can prove my identity to anyone's satisfaction."

The dowager shrugged. "Perhaps you will be fortunate, then. It is simply too bad that your father failed in his duty to claim his title and was then irresponsible enough to remove himself to the colonies. Girls, even the wealthiest, who lack the proper British background are not allowed into Almack's, you know. If you hoped to catch a peer, I'm afraid you are destined to be disappointed."

"I daresay even Lord Blackwold would never consider marrying anyone not approved by the patronesses of that august institution," Hannah replied, unable to stop herself.

"Indeed. I cannot suppose that anyone would believe otherwise."

"Then it should reassure you to know that *I* would never marry a man willing to sell his title to any woman granted a ticket to Almack's."

The dowager's eyes glittered with amusement as she nodded. "That is indeed reassuring. You and I shall undoubtedly set Society on its ear when we arrive in London. You need not attend Almack's to enjoy yourself. It appears the Season will be far less tedious than I feared."

"I'm glad I can provide you with some amusement, then," Hannah said, not bothering to keep the sarcasm out of her voice.

Despite her frustration with Lady Blackwold's attitude, Hannah couldn't help but like her. The dowager seemed to be as fatally honest as Hannah herself, and at least she knew where she stood with her.

She was less sure about Lord Blackwold. One moment she was convinced he was a noble idiot, and the next, she recognized sharp intelligence burning in his brown eyes. But no matter. For the moment, she had a sheltering place to live and a chaperone in the form of the over-honest Lady Blackwold.

That gave her time to regain her feet and determine how to proceed.

The most important thing was to locate her trunk. Since it contained nothing but personal effects that wouldn't interest wreckers, she had high hopes that it might be found, assuming it was not at the bottom of the ocean.

All she had to do was find a way to search the beach.

Chapter Four

"What are your plans, Miss Cowles?" the dowager asked as she followed Hannah out of the dining room, using a cane for balance.

Hannah couldn't help a glance of longing at the staircase, remembering the softness of the pillows on her bed and the warmth of the quilt. If only she could return to her bedroom and spend the rest of the day in bed. Her body ached for sleep, and she had to keep thoughts of all the poor passengers and crew of the *Orion* out of her mind. Grief threatened to overwhelm the fragile walls she was trying to build between herself and the tragedy. Even when she didn't think about the others, tears burned her eyes, threatening to spill over if she relaxed for a moment.

Movement and activity were her only bulwark against crumpling into a sobbing heap on the floor.

"Miss Cowles?" Lady Blackwold repeated, shifting from one foot to the other. A flicker of pain wrinkled her face, but it was gone in an instant.

"I apologize, I was distracted."

"Not by my grandson, I trust."

A short, bitter laugh escaped Hannah. "I was thinking about flotsam and jetsam. Would it be possible to visit the beach? If my trunk managed to come ashore, it would resolve a great many problems."

"Ah, yes, those papers of yours." Lady Blackwold nodded thoughtfully, resting both gnarled hands upon the end of her cane and leaning on it. "Not that a chaperone will do you any good at this point, but I will have a chair brought to the cliffs, so I may watch from there. We have a private path down—I will show you. It is too steep for me, but you are young enough to enjoy the bit of danger it offers."

"Thank you." Hannah touched her gnarled hands, grateful for the suggestion and knowing that Lady Blackwold was not without her own personal discomfort and pains.

"Don't thank me yet, Miss Cowles. There will be others searching the beach. If your trunk did survive, it may have already been taken. The villagers have the right of salvage and are quick to exercise it."

"Then we should hurry." Pacing the wide hallway, Hannah did her best not to nag the plump butler, Mr. Hopwood, or Mary to collect everything Lady Blackwold ordained to be necessary.

The dowager kept calling out items, including a folding chair for her, a blanket for her knees, shawls, hats, gloves, blankets, and a parasol to keep the sun off of her wrinkled cheeks.

At last they set off, going through a library at the back of the house to a set of wide French doors. The flagstone terrace beyond was windswept and bare, and the gardens beyond were equally sere, waiting for the warmth of spring. Although here and there, the long, strap-like green leaves of bulbs were rising, and the sight of new life cheered Hannah.

Lady Blackwold took Hannah's arm and guided her past the clipped boxwood edges of the garden to a meandering path, heading for the rocks. Hannah's heart thudded uncomfortably, dreading the climb down and fearful of what she might find amid the rocks on the beach.

"I will await you here, Miss Cowles," the dowager announced as they neared the downward-curving edge of the sere lawn. "Hopwood, set my chair here." She motioned with a flick of her right hand, and the butler quickly unfolded the chair.

Mary assisted her to sit and carefully tucked the heavy blanket around her knees and a second shawl around her bent shoulders.

"The path is there," Lady Blackwold said, pointing to a dirt trail that led between two black rocks. "Just follow it. It will take you to the beach."

Hannah nodded and walked quickly to the head of the precipitous path. Eyes firmly fixed on the narrow dirt track, she gripped her skirt to keep the wind from whipping it against her legs and tripping her. While she wasn't afraid of heights, the stiff breeze and lack of a handrail made her chest feel tight, and she had to force herself to breathe and move forward, eyes fixed on the narrow, sunken trail.

By the time she reached the beach, she felt flushed and breathless. Locks of her hair whipped across her face, blown by the salt-scented wind roaring in from the sea. Frothy, white-capped waves raced and crashed over the rock-strewn beach, a few still carrying broken pieces of the *Orion* and throwing them against the narrow half-moon of sand.

A few rough-looking men with caps and woolen jackets flapping around them stopped their activities when they saw her. Hannah lifted a hand to wave. One old man with tufts of gray hair sticking out from under his fraying cap touched the brim of his hat and waved back before they returned to their work. They sorted through the detritus to pick up whatever took their fancy and add it to a cache at the base of another trail leading up the cliff at the furthest edge of the beach.

To her surprise, a tall man with a slightly less tattered jacket and cap strolled over to her. "Miss Cowles," Lord Blackwold greeted her. "Come to find your trunk?"

"Yes," she said, lifting her chin and staring at him with a firm gaze. "I'm hoping the contents will save me from absolute ruin."

He grimaced and shook his head. "Too late for that, Flotsam."

"Don't call me that," she replied testily. "I loathe nicknames."

"Too late for that, too. The villagers have decided, and so it shall be."

"And have they also decided that my reputation is in tatters?"

"Well, they definitely feel that a true lady would not be found wandering around at night in a tattered gown. And the tale is, that she was not quite alone."

"Well, I *was* quite alone. And I suppose if I wanted to be considered a proper lady, I would have simply drowned quietly when the *Orion* went down."

"It would certainly have helped," he said blandly. His brown eyes twinkled with amusement. "And think what a romantic story you would have made—a fair young American heiress drowned just eighteen hours before she set foot on the land of her noble father's birth. Brings tears to the eyes, doesn't it?"

"It can still be rectified. I can climb back up the path and fling myself off the edge. Just think what the villagers would say then! Fair young American heiress—"

"Lately of Boston," Blackwold interjected.

"And of unsound mind and distraught after the wreck of the *Orion*, casts herself over the cliff onto the very rocks that destroyed the vessel bringing her to our shores."

"That's the spirit, Miss Cowles! It would be just the thing to repair your ruined reputation, if you can manage it."

Hannah breathed in a sharp, angry breath before she broke down into a small laugh. She smothered her giggles behind one gloved hand and tried to hold on to her annoyance, but it had vanished completely after the absurdity of Lord Blackwold's remarks.

When she looked up, she caught his gaze fixed on her. Flecks of gold glimmered in the depths of his deep brown eyes. His firm mouth quirked, and tiny laugh lines crinkled his tanned skin. The salt air carried the faint scent of his bay soap to her and another, richer scent that made her toes curl in her borrowed shoes.

Her glance was caught by his, and all she could think was, *oh, no!* She hadn't realized how truly attractive he was. Where was the noble idiot she'd considered him to be?

Lady Blackwold had warned her, but she hadn't listened. Now, it felt as if that warning might have come too late.

Her heart thudded in her chest, and she felt her cheeks flame before she tore her gaze away to stare at her feet. Clearing her throat, she said in a light voice, "Unfortunately, it may simply be a case of effrontery and stubbornness, but I wish to continue living, unladylike though that desire is. What's done is done, no matter how convenient a fall from the cliff might be for everyone here." She eyed him, trying to look stern, but still feeling breathless and off-balance. She almost caught at his sleeve when a strong gust of wind hit her. "And I refuse to apologize any further for surviving the wreck."

He smiled and then turned sideways to direct a glance at the other men. "I'm a simple man, Miss Cowles—"

"Oh, I doubt that, Lord Blackwold," she said, interrupting him with a laugh. "I don't believe for a minute that you are the simpleton that you would have others believe you to be. In fact, I think you spend a great deal of time making exceedingly subtle jokes and then laughing at the rest of us when we fail to notice."

He chuckled and shrugged. "Nonetheless, I seem to be too simple to understand the importance of this missing trunk of yours."

"It contains papers—letters of introduction and a letter to a bank so I may withdraw funds transferred here for me. Of course, it is important!"

"Ah, and here I feared you were simply concerned about your lack of gowns," he remarked with a perfectly bland expression on his face.

"I care nothing for gowns," Hannah replied, torn between a strong desire to scream at him and an even stronger urge to laugh. He had some quality of personality that dragged smiles out of her, even when she didn't want to smile, or worse, wasn't even sure if she liked him.

"Evidently."

She smothered another laugh. "You are not simple, unless you mean you are simply a *beast*. I may not be a proper lady, but even I know that a gentleman would never insult a lady's choice of garb."

"No doubt," he agreed jauntily. "But you might explain one small matter to me, if you would. While I agree the papers in the trunk would be important to an American lady named Miss Hannah Cowles, formerly of Boston, I am at a loss to see how they would help you prove that you are she."

"So, you persist in believing that I am an adventuress, taking advantage of the *Orion*'s sinking to assume the identity of an American heiress?"

"It would not be the first time." He shrugged, a distant expression on his face.

He was clearly remembering other women, other times his grandmother had been duped by dishonest females. The thought both saddened and angered her.

"It would be the first time for me, I assure you. But no matter, find the trunk, and I *will* be able to prove who I am."

"How?" He gazed at her, his brown eyes filled with curiosity.

She wavered, wishing she saw warm approval instead of just curiosity in his gold-flecked gaze. She straightened and lifted her chin, forcing her thoughts back to her trunk. There was no need to reveal anything beforehand and risk theft. "You will see, once the trunk is found."

"And if it is never found?"

"Then I must think of some other way to prove to *your* satisfaction that I am not an imposter."

"Imposter? Who is an imposter? You haven't been playacting again, have you, Cousin? A comedy in three parts on the beach?" a man asked from behind Hannah. "Or pretending to be a simpleton barely able to scratch his name?"

She whirled, her long skirts slapping her ankles, to find a well-dressed man stepping off the path. She glanced up to the top of the cliff. Lady Blackwold waved to her, clearly undismayed by the new arrival.

"Cousin," Lord Blackwold acknowledged the stranger.

She looked at Blackwold, her curiosity caught by the lack of emotion in his tone.

He didn't seem to notice her glance. He took a step back to face her and the stranger squarely. "Miss Cowles, may I present my cousin, Mr. Henry Hodges?" He gestured to Hannah. "This is Miss Hannah Cowles, lately of Boston, and a guest of our grandmother."

"And an imposter?" Mr. Hodges grinned to take the sting out of his words. He bent over her hand. "I am charmed and surprised. I had not realized that the dowager knew anyone from the colonies."

Hannah eyed him, from his black hat, worn at a rakish angle, to his fashionable greatcoat, to his shiny boots. He was several inches shorter than Blackwold, with gray eyes instead of brown and well-groomed short hair. His sleek appearance made his taller cousin appear even more bear-like and shaggy, and she couldn't help glancing at Blackwold again in comparison.

The marquess's rumpled appearance brought to mind a man who had just rolled out of his comfortable bed and hadn't had a chance to brush his thick hair or pull on decent clothing. A soft shadow over his strong chin revealed stubble only imperfectly shaved, and that warm, evocative scent hung around him that she'd noticed before. Bay soap, a touch of leather, and salt air all mingled together. The fragrance made her want to lean closer, close her eyes, and breathe deeply.

When he caught her gaze, a gentle smile curved his mouth. His heavy-lidded eyes seemed a trifle drowsy before he turned away to watch the men working along the beach. With his profile to her, his expression was more bemused than alert. And yet she had the sense that Blackwold saw everything that transpired. One would be making a serious mistake to believe his placid demeanor indicated he was unaware, or unintelligent as she first assumed.

Mouth dry, she pushed the thoughts away. Without even considering it, Hannah took a step closer to Lord

Blackwold. She couldn't help a quick look at Hodges's hands as she did so.

He wore black leather gloves.

Her gaze flashed to Blackwold's large hands. A white scar marred his right hand, running from the knuckle of his index finger to his wrist. A heavy ring adorned that hand, as well. Her breathing stuttered.

Her hands caught at the ends of her shawl and pulled the soft wool more tightly around her shoulders. She hugged herself against the nervous flutter chilling her limbs. She couldn't be sure—not entirely—but the ring on Blackwold's index finger looked remarkably similar to the one she'd seen during the storm. The one the wrecker had worn—the man who'd ordered Officer Trent's death.

Had she seen a scar? She concentrated but couldn't remember—all she could see in the flaring, golden light of the storm lantern was that ring.

His voice? Surely... No. The storm winds and waves had muted and distorted the man's voice to the point where she couldn't be sure. She couldn't remember anything except the roar of the surf and the sting of the salt water against her face. All she had as a clue was that ring.

Chapter Five

The sand seemed to shift beneath Hannah's feet. She glanced up to find both men watching her.

"What brings you to our fair shores, Miss Cowles?" Mr. Hodges asked, his gray eyes revealing nothing but polite enquiry.

"I—my father was born here. In England." Her words stumbled over each other, making them sound inane. *Silly*. She took a deep breath, torn between her publicly stated reasons and her private dreams.

Her longing to see where her father had been born, to find a true home—someplace where she could settle down and not be yanked from one inn to another—tightened her throat. That was her cherished reason for her trip, though she kept it hidden for fear that if she spoke the words out loud, it would evaporate like the dew under the hot sun and remain forever out of her reach.

But her soul ached for her own place in the world. Her father had always blithely claimed that one's heart made any place a home and had never wanted to settle down. He'd always hungered to see what was down the road or over the next hill, and his wife agreed.

Hannah was different, though. She hated the constant travel, never feeling like she belonged anywhere, but she'd remained silent. She'd never told her parents that she was tired of their ceaseless travels and wanted to stay in one place, where she could find friends and contentment in the familiar things surrounding her.

While she loved both of them, they were different. They disliked the ordinary and craved the excitement of the unknown territory that lay just beyond the next hill. But she craved a routine—a commonplace life—and friends she could actually visit, instead of simply writing letters to them.

And now, she wondered if the wreck of the *Orion* had destroyed even that small, private dream.

"I see. Was your father acquainted with Lady Blackwold, then?" Mr. Hodges asked politely, turning to wave at the dowager.

She waved back with her handkerchief, the feathers of her bonnet bobbing as she nodded.

"No. At least, I am not aware of any acquaintance between our families," Hannah answered, acutely aware of the closeness of Blackwold.

She couldn't trust him, she reminded herself sharply. He wore that ring.

In fact, she couldn't trust any of them. Her gaze bounced from one man to the other before coming to rest on a small, smooth stone near her right foot. Her mind raced furiously, sorting through the facts she thought she knew. But the facts warred with her feelings.

Despite his doubts about her character, she'd liked Blackwold. He intrigued her with his sense of humor and his bearlike appearance seemed more endearing than frightening. But she knew no more of him than he knew of her.

He wears a ring! Her mind insisted.

"She was on the *Orion*," Blackwold said, stepping further away and eyeing the men laboring on the beach. "If that answers your questions, Hodges."

"Ah, I see." Mr. Hodges nodded and touched her forearm lightly with sympathy. "I am so sorry. I heard the news this morning. It must have been a terrible ordeal." He shivered with sympathy. "Should you not be resting?"

Hannah shrugged and looked away, lowering her arm to avoid his lingering touch.

"Well, it shows great strength of character that you are here and able to view the sad evidence of your recent tragedy." Mr. Hodges paused to adjust the cuff on one sleeve and brush off a speck of sand. "And, I beg your pardon, but did I hear mention of a trunk?"

"Yes—my trunk. I was hoping to find it, if it washed ashore. It has my name, Hannah Cowles, engraved on it." She studied the thin, frayed jackets of the scavengers. "I am not concerned about the gowns; if the villagers want them, I will not object. I simply want the trunk itself."

"Generous and intriguing..." Mr. Hodges murmured. His eyes glittered strangely, and a small, secretive smile curled his lips. "Shall we see if such a trunk has been found?" He held out his arm to her. "Our industrious scavengers may have seen it, or pulled it out of the sea." His contempt for the men on the beach came through clearly in the curl of his thin upper lip and emphasis of the word *scavengers*.

When she glanced at Lord Blackwold, he was already walking away to join the villagers.

He's one of them. It must have been him, last night. And how many of the other men scattered over the beach were there, as well, clubbing the survivors?

White and gray gulls shrieked overhead, eyeing the intruders on the beach and landing on nearby rocks to search for tempting bits of sea life left behind by the storm. They were scavengers, too, fighting and screaming over remains of the *Orion*.

The thought sickened her, and she swallowed, forcing down the knot in her throat. Slowly, with reluctance, she slipped her hand through Mr. Hodges's elbow and let him escort her to the growing pile of goods the men had collected from the wreckage.

One large, aggressive gull kept landing on the pile, only to flap away when one of the men approached.

"Where did you come ashore, Miss Cowles?" Mr. Hodges asked as he assisted her around rocks and broken planks from the *Orion*.

"Come ashore?" she repeated the question, stopping to glance around. "Not here—I must have been swept further south and away from the house."

"One of our villagers must have assisted you; it would have been difficult to avoid the rocks during a storm." He shivered elaborately at the thought. "I am accounted to be a decent swimmer, but even I would have had difficulties finding my way to shore safely anywhere except this small scrap of beach."

"No one assisted me," she replied sharply. "I saw no one—if anyone was trying to assist us, the storm hid them from view. I had to do the best I could with a broken spar to aid me."

"Regrettable," Mr. Hodges murmured. "I'm sure you would have gained a much better view of our quaint little village and its inhabitants if they had been able to assist in your rescue. We are not a callous and inhospitable race, I assure you, and I sincerely regret our failure."

"There is nothing to regret. I'm sure they would have come to my aid if they'd seen me." Even if that aid consisted of a club to the head.

As they neared the pile of refuse, the gull flapped away again. Hannah's heart twisted as she recognized bits and pieces that belonged to the crew and passengers aboard the *Orion*. A small wooden chest with brass hinges had been thrown heedlessly midway up the left side of the pile.

It had belonged to her companion, Mrs. Lawrence.

Pulse racing, Hannah paused, almost tripping over a broken board. Should she try to claim it? Mrs. Lawrence had no family, no one to notify of her death, and no one to care what happened to the contents of that small box.

"Do you see something you recognize?" Mr. Hodges asked, turning to look at her. Speculation turned his eyes to smooth gray stones, like those washed onto the beach by the tide.

She glanced away, rubbing her arms with cold hands. Fear tasted sour in her mouth as she heard the low murmurs of the men around her, men who cast enigmatic glances at her as they worked. How many of them had been present last night? What would they do if she tried to claim a few of the items she recognized?

Before she could decide how to answer Mr. Hodges, Blackwold loped over and picked up the small box. He flashed her a shy grin before striding over.

"Something of yours?" Blackwold held the box out to her.

A few of the men paused, scowling in their direction.

She shook her head and clasped her hands at her waist. "It belongs to Mrs. Lawrence—my companion." Her voice broke, and she pressed her fingers against her lips, struggling to regain her composure. Warm tears stung her cheeks, and she blinked rapidly. "*Belonged* to Mrs. Lawrence, that is," she said in a stronger voice.

Mr. Hodges glanced away, pretending to be fascinated by the efforts of three men to drag a large crate to shore, thereby giving her a moment of privacy.

"I'm sorry," Blackwold said, thrusting the box at her again. "A keepsake, perhaps?"

"The villagers may want it. To sell," she replied, struggling for a light tone. Chest tight, she tried to take a deep breath, but it came out as a shuddering sigh before she pressed her hand to her mouth again.

One of Blackwold's brows rose. "Is it valuable, then?"

"The box, perhaps. Mrs. Lawrence—" She broke off again, swallowed, and cleared her throat. The sharp pain of her companion's death cut deeply—too deeply to let her say her name easily. Suddenly, she felt terribly alone. Mrs. Lawrence had been with her for so long that she could barely remember a time when her calm presence hadn't been there to give her guidance when she needed it and hug her when she desperately craved comfort.

She cleared her throat and lifted her chin. "My companion didn't have much of value. I don't know what she kept in that little chest."

Without asking, Blackwold reached over and plucked a long, elaborate hatpin out of her hat. Her hands fluttered up to hold her borrowed bonnet in place, sudden anger whipping through her in outrage at his overly familiar gesture.

But her protest died on her lips as he delicately inserted the pin in the brass lock and wriggled it. His first attempt to open the box failed. He frowned in concentration before a sudden click rewarded his efforts.

"There you are." He held the wooden box out to her with his left hand and shoved the hatpin back into her hat with his right.

Once again, her hands flew to her head as her bonnet slid back under his assault, and she readjusted the pin to hold the hat more securely on her head before accepting the small box.

Staring down at the box, she calmed herself. *I won't cry—I won't!* She flipped open the lid to find a small bundle of papers inside. They were damp, and the ink had seeped through in a few places where the sea water had moistened the paper.

"Just letters," she said, glancing up. From her husband—Hannah felt sure, remembering her companion's few remarks concerning her loss.

Blackwold was studying the growing pile of salvaged goods while his cousin was looking at her with a strange expression of distaste. Or perhaps scorn. Hannah couldn't decide, but it made her feel embarrassed about the show of emotion she'd been helpless to control.

She plucked the letters from the box and held them against her. She could read them later, in private. "Here. The others can have the box, if it is of value to them." She shoved the box into Blackwold's hand, once again noticing the ring on his finger. A chill slipped down her neck, and she looked away, fixing her gaze on the gray, restless waves pounding against the rocks and sending up spumes of frothy white foam.

More gulls screamed and wheeled above them, their wings flashing white against the blue-gray sky.

"Surely, you mean to keep it," Mr. Hodges said. "The villagers have salvaged enough from the sea. That small box is of no use to them." His thin lips twisted. "Since it is clearly empty of any valuables."

"Bereft of valuables for *them,* perhaps," Hannah replied abruptly before pressing her lips shut.

"Of course," Mr. Hodges said smoothly, brushing one hand down the front of his coat. "Your tender sensibilities do you credit, Miss Cowles."

Instead of feeling flattered, Hannah felt a surge of irritation at Mr. Hodges's remark. He clearly intended it to be sympathetic, but it felt condescending. Nonetheless, she forced herself to smile and nod her head in thanks, precisely like the empty-headed English lady he clearly expected her to be.

Perhaps Mr. Hodges, like his grandmother and cousin, had an unfortunate way of expressing his thoughts. She shook her head. She was so tired and overset with warring emotions that she might have interpreted his words in the worst way possible.

She doubted it, but it remained a remote possibility.

Without explanation, Blackwold thrust the box back into her hand. The ring on his finger flashed in the gray, wintery light. Once again, she felt a stab of deep fear and doubt, although her hand closed automatically upon the box.

Could this amiable man really be the same one who had given orders for Officer Trent to be clubbed? It seemed impossible. She would rather believe it of Mr. Hodges than Lord Blackwold.

The marquess certainly appeared to be on good terms with the villagers, though. While she could not prove that any of the shabbily dressed men had participated in the events of the night before, it did seem likely.

Before she could express her thanks, Blackwold turned away. "Turner!"

A gray whiskered man straightened, lifted his cap, and ran his forearm over his glistening bald head. Then he moved toward them with a rolling, bandy-legged gait. "Yes, my lord?"

"A guinea for the box. Agreed?" Blackwold held out a coin.

The old man's pale blue eyes locked on the box with the air of a connoisseur judging a fine painting. He pursed his wrinkled lips and scratched the rough gray whiskers of his cheek.

"There was nothing of value in it except some old letters," Blackwold pointed out before pulling back the proffered coin a few inches. "At any rate, you would have sold it, so it should not matter to you if I am the purchaser. But if you are not interested..." His hand holding the coin descended toward his pocket.

"Aye, my lord. A guinea would suit me fine. Just fine." Turner held out a grubby hand. When Blackwold tossed the coin to him, Turner caught it with an adept movement and shoved it into his pocket in the blink of an eye. "Thank you, my lord."

The old man gave the box one last, speculative glance.

Before he could move back to the pile of salvage, Hannah stopped him. "Mr. Turner," she said. "Do you know if anyone has seen a trunk? It is a round trunk, covered in leather, with brass tacks and iron handles. The tacks on the lid form a design incorporating my initials, HCC. It is unmistakable."

"Can't say as I've seen it, Miss." Turner shrugged and took a sideways step toward the rapidly increasing stack of goods.

"Inform me if you do," Blackwold said.

Turner eyed him and scratched his whiskered cheek again.

"For suitable recompense, of course," Blackwold added.

"Aye, my lord." Turner grinned and ambled off toward a fresh pile of detritus rolling over the beach, dragged forward and back by the waves.

"Thank you, Lord Blackwold. That was very generous of you—too generous," Hannah said, wishing she didn't feel like a poor relative being tossed a few scraps. She slipped the letters back into the box.

"I'll get a locksmith to replace the lock. Tomorrow," he replied, his gaze fixed on the restless, dark gray ocean.

"There is no need," she started to say, but she was speaking to his broad back.

Lord Blackwold's long stride carried him quickly down the beach.

Mr. Hodges touched her arm. "Perhaps you will permit me to escort you back to the house? Although you are as lovely as ever, this must have been a strain for you. You must need rest to refresh yourself." His thin mouth twisted into a smile. "My grandmother is sure to demand your attendance at supper, so you may not have another opportunity for privacy today."

"Thank you, you are very kind." Hannah allowed him to draw her back to the path and help her to ascend, although she'd felt safer on her own without his hand in the center of her back encouraging her forward.

"This trunk you mentioned," he said in an offhand way.

The path was too precipitous for her to glance over her shoulder at him, though she wished she could see the expression on his face. "Yes?"

"You must have some valuable belongings in it. It must be distressing to lose everything to the storm."

"Yes—but it is not merely the loss of my gowns that concerns me." Her jaws clamped shut. She must have explained the matter of her trunk and documents a dozen times, and the subject was becoming exceedingly annoying. "There are papers inside—documents that establish that I am indeed Hannah Cowles and that grant me access to the funds my lawyer in Boston transferred for me to the Bank of England. On Threadneedle Street."

The silence behind her made the vulnerable nape of her neck tingle.

They were within ten yards of the top of the cliff when Mr. Hodges said, "Your chest must be found, then, Miss Cowles. I would not have you left impoverished by the storm." He gripped her elbow as they stepped onto the firm grassy ground.

When she glanced at him, he smiled at her.

"Though I doubt anyone truly questions who you are," he added.

"Clearly, you underestimate the suspicious nature of Lord Blackwold and the dowager."

He laughed and shook his head over the foibles of his relatives as he led her over to Lady Blackwold.

"I see you have met another of my grandsons," the dowager said with a grin. She held out a gloved hand to Mr. Hodges and drew him close enough to kiss his cheek as he bent over her hand. "Handsome devil, isn't he?"

Hannah murmured a vague reply, not wishing to get into a discussion about the relative appearance of Mr. Hodges versus his cousin, Lord Blackwold.

"Help me to the house, Henry. This breeze has chilled me to the bone."

"I hope you have not caught a chill, Grandmother. I cannot imagine what possessed you to sit here at the edge of the cliff for so long." Mr. Hodges assisted his grandmother to rise and tucked her hand through his elbow before he thrust out his other arm for Hannah.

She swallowed back a sigh.

Mr. Hodges was trying so hard to be kind and gentlemanly to her, and he was the only one who'd neither questioned who she was nor insisted she was ruined simply because she had the misfortune to survive the wreck. But as perverse as it was, she preferred his ridiculous cousin who clearly failed to trust her and was most likely a cold-hearted wrecker who'd murdered the rest of the survivors.

"I wished to see if they'd found anything of interest on the beach," his grandmother replied loftily.

"And did they?" Mr. Hodges asked, obviously humoring her.

"Not that I could see. Although Miss Cowles has brought back a box of some sort." The dowager peered around Mr. Hodges to grin at Hannah. "Is that the chest you were so anxious to find?"

"No." Hannah cleared her throat at the sudden stab of pain over the loss of Mrs. Lawrence. "It belonged to my companion. And friend. I didn't see my trunk among the wreckage."

"Don't give up hope, Miss Cowles," Mr. Hodges said. "It may yet appear. Tomorrow morning, I will personally go to the village and enquire about it. Someone may have already transported it there."

"I would sincerely appreciate that, Mr. Hodges."

As they neared the terrace doors, Hannah paused to allow Mr. Hodges to assist his grandmother to ascend the shallow steps and enter the house. She glanced out across the wide expanse of the sere gardens and lawn, noting once again the proud spears of green thrusting their way through the earth.

Dark clouds were gathering over the gray Atlantic, and a cold, brisk wind was whipping the waves into a froth. Gulls swooped and screeched, flashing white, black, and gray against the sky. From a distance, they were beautiful and sleek, despite their harsh noise. Over the ocean, the vast expanse of sky grew blacker as she watched.

Another storm was brewing. Hannah drew her shawl more closely around her shoulders and smiled gratefully at Mr. Hodges as he helped her into the house.

"Will you stay for supper, Henry? It will not be much— we had dinner earlier, and there will only be cold meats and whatever was left," the dowager asked as she began the tedious process of removing her bonnet, gloves, and multiple shawls. One after the other, she handed the items to the butler, who already had his arms full with Mr. Hodges coat and hat.

"If I may," he bowed to her, grinning.

Lady Blackwold snorted and gave his forearm a light slap. "He is a charming rogue, isn't he, Miss Cowles? One can never be sure what he will do."

What was clear to Hannah was that the dowager had a soft spot for Henry Hodges, unaccountable though it was. He was far too glib and too sleek for Hannah's taste. In some strange way, with his gray coat and black gloves, he reminded her of the gulls wheeling over the beach outside.

As he drew off his gloves and placed them on the top of the pile of garments in Hopwood's arms, a ring on his right hand flashed. Hannah stared at it, a shiver trembling down her back.

"What is it, Miss Cowles?" the dowager asked. "You have gone quite pale."

"Just a draft from the door," Hannah replied quickly, her gaze locked on the ring.

The piece of jewelry appeared to be identical to the one Lord Blackwold wore.

"The day has grown quite cold. I suspect we shall have another storm this evening." The dowager patted Mr. Hodges's arm. "You must stay the night, Henry. You cannot ride home in the rain."

"It is not that far, but I shall do as you wish." He smiled and kissed his grandmother's wrinkled cheek.

When she turned to Hannah, she caught the direction of Hannah's gaze. With a grin remarkably similar to Mr. Hodges's, Lady Blackwold said, "You have noticed the family ring, I see. Each of my sons wore one—a conceit of my late husband's to give each of our sons a ring with the griffin's head from our family seal." A shadow of pain crossed her face, deepening the wrinkles around her mouth and sad eyes. "My two eldest sons are gone, so Adam and Henry have inherited their rings."

"Naturally, as the son of the second son, the jewels in my ring are merely rubies. Blackwold's has diamonds," Mr. Hodges said in a deprecating tone as he held up his ring and tilted it to catch the candlelight. The griffin's eyes flashed blood red.

Hannah moved closer to the fire, crackling merrily in the library's wide fireplace. "So, there are two rings," she murmured, relieved that the cruel man on the beach need not have been Lord Blackwold after all. Some of the tension gripping her chest eased.

"Four," Lady Blackwold said. "I had four sons, and two are still living. Brian has the sapphire-eyed griffin and Carter—the youngest—has the topaz." Her eyes brightened, and she smiled. "Brian was a captain in the navy—we were all so proud of him."

"Indeed," Mr. Hodges said, gazing at the fire, his brows drawn together over the bridge of his nose.

Hannah thought he looked less proud of his uncle than mildly irritated.

"And his daughter, Georgina, is due to come to me at the end of the week," the dowager continued, her voice rising with pleasure and excitement. "We will be leaving shortly thereafter for London. I am to present her to Society as her mother—poor, weak thing that she was—died when she was born." She winked at Hannah, her hands fluttering to the ribbons of her lacy cap. "And I trust you will join us, Miss Cowles?"

"I—well, perhaps—if my trunk is found." Hannah stumbled over her words. What was she going to do if her trunk was never found? She couldn't cling to Lady Blackwold forever.

Lady Blackwold caught her grandson's arm. "Did I tell you that Miss Cowles is the daughter of Richard Cowles?" Her gray brows rose, touching the fringe of gray curls framing her forehead.

Mr. Hodges smiled politely, but his eyes were devoid of comprehension.

Lady Blackwold's grip on his sleeve tightened, and she shook his arm. "Richard *Cowles*," she repeated. "That silly man who decided that wandering about in foreign parts was more important than his title. *The Baron—Lord Rothguard*! Or he *would* have been Lord Rothguard, if he'd bothered to apply for his title."

"Ah," Mr. Hodges nodded and gently pried his arm loose from his grandmother's grip. "I begin to see the importance of this trunk, Miss Cowles."

"I am not interested in the title." Hannah crossed her arms. "I merely want to settle all questions concerning my identity."

"Of course," Mr. Hodges agreed politely, though the speculative gleam had returned to his eyes. "Well, I beg your forgiveness, but I have other matters to attend to."

"You will join us for dinner, though, will you not?" his grandmother replied swiftly.

Mr. Hodges smiled and gave his grandmother a reassuring kiss on the cheek. "Of course, my dearest. How can I resist such charming company?"

A flush of pleasure brought color to the dowager's round cheeks. She grinned and said, "You are a tease and flatterer, but you have my permission to abandon us ladies to our own devices."

He bowed to her and Hannah and strode out, shutting the door behind him.

When Hannah turned back to Lady Blackwold, the dowager's gaze was fixed on her. "Now Henry would not mind a bit of scandal, Miss Cowles. It would not matter to him in the least, assuming you can locate this trunk of yours."

Hannah felt her cheeks grow warm and stepped closer to the fire, hoping the dowager would believe it was the heat from the flames that brought the color to her face.

The last thing she wanted to do was to attract Mr. Hodges, if that was what the dowager alluded to in her comment about her grandson. Hannah felt no interest in him and wasn't about to sacrifice her freedom for the dubious safety of marriage with someone she barely knew.

"Come, Miss Cowles, it must have occurred to you—you must consider your future."

"Perhaps my trunk will never be found," Hannah replied demurely. She smiled at the dowager. "Perhaps I could become your companion."

The dowager laughed. "You are not placid enough to engage in that employment, even if I wished it." Her face seemed to crumple, though, and her eyes grew sad as she moved over to sit in a chair by the fire. Leaning on her cane, she waved to the wing chair next to hers. "Please sit, my dear. I am a silly old woman at times, as you already know." She sighed and shook her head. "I wish I could offer you better gowns than my old cast-offs. If I had the dressing of you, you would look magnificent. But Blackwold keeps me on a strict allowance." Her voice drifted off as she stared into the crackling flames.

Reaching over, Hannah gave the dowager's wrist a squeeze. Despite the dowager's sharp tongue and bluster, she was clearly lonely and sad. Hannah couldn't forget Blackwold's claim that his grandmother had been hurt before—cheated by other women who just wanted to get what they could from an old woman, who was clearly too kind-hearted and generous for her own good. Her sharp words were merely a thin disguise for a tender heart.

Loneliness had made her easy prey, and it bothered Hannah deeply that Blackwold thought she was of the same stamp as the tricksters who had taken advantage of Lady Blackwold and left her nearly destitute.

"Lady Blackwold, it does not matter to me in the least. You have been very generous to me when I am virtually a stranger to you. I am exceedingly grateful to you, and am very pleased with the wardrobe you've granted me."

The dowager sniffed, holding her handkerchief up to her nose, and laughed sadly. "It is little enough. It is simply too bad that Henry has such a superb eye for fashion. He will surely recognize my old gowns, and I'm sorry for it. Still, you are a handsome girl, despite your scrapes and bruises." Her eyes gleamed in the firelight. "We must have our lawyer look into this title of yours—it may yet be salvageable."

When Hannah opened her mouth to protest, the dowager slapped her wrist.

"Oh, *you* cannot claim it—you are only a female, after all. But I have heard of cases... Are you the only living child of Richard Cowles?"

"Yes, but—"

"Excellent. I have heard of cases where the husband of the last child remaining alive might apply for and be granted a title." Her smile widened, and she clapped her hands before clasping them tightly in her lap. "It would be a marvelous thing for Henry to claim a title—even the title of baron. And he would be an excellent husband, my dear. Very considerate and exceedingly fashionable. You could do far worse."

"I'm sure I could," Hannah replied in a strangled voice. Suddenly, she hoped her trunk might never be found. "But that would only be possible if I could prove I am the daughter of Richard Cowles beyond all doubt."

"Naturally, my dear. But once Henry is made aware of what might be gained, I am very sure he shall comb the village most diligently. We will find this missing trunk. I have no doubt of it."

"Or perhaps I should concentrate on learning how to behave as a proper companion," Hannah said. "Which strikes me as a much more practical solution."

The dowager laughed. "Nonsense. Your reputation is in tatters, thanks to my gossiping coachman and the villagers. No one wants a scandalous companion. But a wife—a touch of scandal would not bother anyone in the least—particularly the wife of a baron. After all, you have no need to apply to those stuffy patronesses of Almack's if you are already engaged to be married. You would have security and a home—it would be ideal."

"Ideal," Hannah repeated in a faint voice, much of her previous sympathy for the dowager fading.

Dinner was an informal affair and, feeling drained, Hannah excused herself as quickly as possible to retire to her room. Unfortunately, when she awoke the next day, she felt just as exhausted as she'd been the previous night, and an ache hovered behind her eyes and in all her joints.

The dowager was pleased, however, that Henry decided to spend the day at Blackrock. As if sensing Hannah's dilemma, Mary allowed her to assist in altering more of the dowager's old gowns, saving Hannah from the responsibility of entertaining him for several hours.

By evening, her eyes burned, the ache in her head had spread to her joints, but Hannah's attempts to excuse herself from dinner proved fruitless. The dowager simply ignored all of Hannah's efforts.

"Well, it is getting late—we should prepare for dinner. Thank goodness you still have your jewels. Henry may not notice you are wearing one of my gowns if your neck is graced with diamonds and emeralds." She frowned thoughtfully, her forehead creasing. "Although perhaps that is too much for an unwed girl... Pearls! You must wear your pearls. They are beautiful enough for even the most discerning eye and entirely appropriate for a young woman. You must wear your pearls, Miss Cowles!"

"Yes, Lady Blackwold," Hannah replied, feeling doomed. She almost wished she hadn't stumbled onto the road and been rescued by the dowager. Drowning was reputed to be a gentle death, after all.

She helped the dowager to rise. Lady Blackwold leaned heavily against Hannah's arm as they crossed the room and headed for the staircase.

"I truly wish I had a new gown to give you," the dowager said as they climbed the stairs.

A new gown was the last thing Hannah wanted. "Don't worry, Lady Blackwold. There is no need for such extravagance. After all, I may never be able to prove who I am."

"Do not be absurd, Miss Cowles. We shall, and we will do so."

Was it too late to quietly walk into the ocean? She didn't want to be a churlish and ungrateful guest, but suddenly, she dreaded dinner at Blackrock.

Chapter Six

Bemused, Hannah stared at the pale rose silk dress that Mary had laid out on the bed. The gown was lovely, despite the suggestion in the lines that it had been remade from a gown that originated in the previous century.

"Lady Blackwold sent this for you to wear to dinner tonight," Mary said in a toneless voice. Her downcast gaze seemed to be focused on the tips of her black shoes, and she clasped her red chapped hands in front of her crisp, white apron.

"Thank you," Hannah responded for want of a better reply. A sense of being maneuvered into place assailed her.

Certainly, the dowager had made it clear earlier that, while Hannah's reputation might be too damaged for acceptance by Polite Society or her titled grandson, she was not so ruined that she wouldn't do for her other grandson, Henry Hodges. Particularly since the possibility existed that Henry might obtain the title of baron if he ignored the deficiencies in Hannah's reputation.

What the dowager failed to realize was that if Mr. Hodges could gain a title that way, so could any other gentleman Hannah cared to consider.

Which might make her very popular, despite her damaged reputation.

She studied the silk dress with distaste. She had no desire to flirt with Mr. Hodges or attempt to attract his attention. Earlier in the day, her feelings concerning that gentleman had been lukewarm, at best, when he insisted she leave her sewing for a walk in the garden. She neither craved his company nor disliked him.

Now, however, since the dowager's inexplicable decision to throw Hannah at his head, she felt a distinct distaste for both him and the silk dress.

"The dress will suit you," Mary said grudgingly as she reached out to smooth a small wrinkle out of the softly glimmering fabric. "With your fair coloring and all."

"I'm not sure I wish to wear it."

Mary stared at her, her mouth hanging open. "Miss?"

Turning away, Hannah glanced at the gowns neatly folded on the shelves of the open wardrobe. Her response had been churlish—beneath her. "Never mind." Hannah sighed. "It is lovely. Lady Blackwold is too generous."

"Yes, she be that, Miss."

At last, something on which they could both agree.

Hannah was beginning to realize that she was unlikely to ever make a friend out of the taciturn maid, but she had to admit that Mary never let her personal feelings—whatever they might be—interfere with her performance of her job.

After helping Hannah into her dress, Mary wrapped a linen towel around Hannah's shoulders, and with extraordinarily gentle strokes of the brush, created a simple but becoming hairstyle. She swept Hannah's hair up into a fashionable knot, threaded with a pink ribbon that matched the silk gown, and created cascades of delicate ringlets on either side of Hannah's face.

Gazing into the mirror, Hannah caught the maid's reflected gaze and smiled. "You have done a beautiful job with very poor material, Mary. You are to be commended." She turned her head from one side to the other to view the results. "I don't believe I have ever looked better."

"Thank you, Miss." Mary removed the linen cloth from around Hannah's neck and busied herself putting everything away. "You'd best be getting along to the sitting room—Lady Blackwold will be waiting."

A sigh escaped from Hannah as she stood and shook out her dress. Her pearl earrings swayed, and her fingers went to the matching necklace. Its pearly sheen echoed the lustrous silk of her dress, and a few pearls picked up a touch of the pale rose, giving the necklace richness and warmth.

The bruises that had developed on her back and hips after being buffeted by the storm were invisible under her elegant dress, but they reminded her of their existence whenever she moved. Her headache made her feel too ill to eat, but she had to at least try. She cast a lingering glance at the bed before she took a deep breath, straightened her back, and walked out of her bedchamber.

Dinner turned out to be much less tedious than Hannah expected. When Blackwold appeared, his neat appearance caused a moment of stunned silence. His valet had worked miracles for the marquess's evening attire was immaculate, his neckcloth was well-knotted, and even his thick hair had been brushed until it gleamed.

The flutter in Hannah's stomach made her clasp her hands together tightly and stare down, afraid of what her eyes might reveal.

Once they recovered from the surprise, the dowager and Henry Hodges vied to outdo each other with amusing stories of their experiences in London.

To Hannah's dismay, course after course was served. Oysters and a thick, aromatic fish soup were followed by a venison roast, larded with bacon, crispy-skinned roasted potatoes, and asparagus in a delicate cream sauce laced with sherry. By the time the final course of dried fruit and cheese appeared, Hannah could only sip her Madeira and hope that no one noticed that she failed to take any of the proffered delicacies.

As they picked over the final course, a sidelong glance at Blackwold made Hannah grin. She bit her lower lip to avoid laughing.

A thick lock of hair hung over his brow and somehow, his neckcloth seemed to be slowly unraveling itself from its previous careful arrangement. The top button of his waistcoat had also come undone, though she could not imagine how, for the button was still tightly sewn to the pale blue and silver-embroidered silk.

The fluttering sensation she'd experienced earlier returned. There was something endearing in his increasing untidiness, and a feeling of warmth filled her.

"Shall we leave the men to their secrets?" Lady Blackwold asked, pressing her palms against the tabletop as she stood.

"Of course," Hannah replied, flushing. Had the dowager noticed Hannah's glances at Blackwold?

She felt embarrassed and flustered. The fingers of her right hand brushed over her pearls, playing over their smooth, warm surface. Like a child unable to resist the one thing she had been denied, she couldn't seem to stop surreptitiously gazing at the marquess. In fact, she was worse than any schoolroom miss besotted by her brother's tutor, she reprimanded herself.

Thankfully, the dowager either didn't notice, or chose to ignore Hannah's blushes. She took Hannah's arm and drew her to the sitting room, continuing a rambling story about her first Season in London, where she appeared to have been the toast of the town and quite ensorcelled at least a dozen fashionable young men.

"I must say, you are looking very well this evening, Miss Cowles. Mary has quite outdone herself," Lady Blackwold said as she sat with a gusty sigh in the red damask wing chair nearest the fire.

"Yes. She is a very skilled maid."

"Have you considered what I said earlier?"

Hannah's brow wrinkled as she sat down in the chair next to her. "What you said earlier?"

"About my grandson. Henry. He is much taken with you, I believe." The dowager laughed and wriggled her small feet with delight. "I knew that gown would suit you and that Henry would notice. And those delicious pearls— you could not have chosen more wisely. Well done, girl."

Hannah's hands tightened on the armrests. She deliberately released her hold and clasped them gently in her lap. "I do not wish to lead him—or you—on, Lady Blackwold. I appreciate the gown and everything you have done for me, but I have no wish to marry—"

"No wish to marry!" The dowager's voice rose. She frowned at Hannah. "You cannot understand what lies ahead of you, if you do not marry." Her wrinkles smoothed away as a pensive look entered her face. "Marriage is not without its terrors, certainly. So many girls die before their time. Childbirth—it is difficult, as you no doubt know. I can understand and sympathize if you are frightened. But there are worse things. To be old and alone..." A shudder went through her. "You cannot want that. At least I have my family—my sons and grandsons. I am not entirely alone."

Hannah nodded, but despite Lady Blackwold's words, she sensed that the dowager did feel alone, despite her large family. Alone and unwanted, living at Blackrock on sufferance because she had no place else to go.

While her grandsons were polite and cared for her well-being, they had their own lives and affairs, often leaving the dowager to spend her days without company. Although Hannah had only been there a short time, she'd gotten the impression that Lady Blackwold often ate her meals alone, as well, attended to by silent servants.

Hannah leaned forward and gave the dowager's arm a squeeze. "I understand, but there is time, is there not? I am just turned twenty, after all. And you must be prepared if I am unable to prove who I am. You would not want Mr. Hodges to marry a nobody—a virtual stranger from a foreign country."

"A colony—not so foreign," the dowager answered with a sad smile. Her hands twisted together before she winced and placed them gently in her lap.

"A *former* colony and quite foreign in all the ways that matter, I assure you."

Lady Blackwold smiled and patted Hannah's knee. "You are a kind girl—when you wish to be. So, we will be patient and see what transpires. We are all going to London in a week. Just as soon as my son can spare Georgina." A mischievous gleam lit her eyes. "And perhaps my Henry will find a titled heiress from the latest crop of girls at Almack's."

"Perhaps he will, and I wish him all the best if he does."

The dowager laughed. "We shall see if you sing the same song when that happens, Miss Cowles. You would not be the first woman to discover too late that she now wants what another possesses."

Rubbing the spot between her brows, Hannah took a deep breath. The heat from the fire had made her drowsy and eased some of the bruises and aches she still felt from the storm's buffeting. She smiled tiredly at the dowager and changed the subject, encouraging her to talk about her own past when she went to London herself for her first Season.

The dowager reminisced happily enough for the next twenty minutes, while Hannah's limbs grew heavier and heavier. Her chin drooped, and she jerked in her chair when one of the logs in the fire crumbled on the fireirons, sending up a shower of gold and red sparks just visible above the top edge of the embroidered fire screen.

If she was to stay awake any longer, she needed a breath of bracing fresh air.

"Will you excuse me for a moment, Lady Blackwold? It is so warm in here that I feel the need for a breath of air."

"Certainly, my dear. You may go out on the terrace—you should be safe enough there, and I will be able to see you through the doors." Leaning forward, she shrugged out of her warm, cashmere shawl and held it out. "Take my shawl. The wind from the sea never lets up, I'm afraid, so you will need it."

"I have a shawl—"

"Pshaw," the dowager said, interrupting her. "You will need more than that flimsy thing. It may be becoming, but that shawl is more appropriate for May than February."

Hannah clamped her mouth shut and took the shawl, avoiding the obvious rejoinder that the dowager herself had given Mary the clothing Hannah was wearing this evening, so she could hardly complain that it was inappropriate for the season.

However, Hannah's exasperation with Lady Blackwold was tempered by a strong urge to laugh. The dowager's mood was nothing if not mercurial.

"I will only be outside for a minute," Hannah replied. "Thank you for the shawl."

The dowager waved her away and transferred her gaze to the crackling fire painting dancing patterns of light and dark on the embroidered fire screen.

Just as the dowager predicted, a chilly wind blew toward the house from the cliffs. Shivering, Hannah wrapped the extra shawl around her shoulders, grateful for the additional warmth. The soft folds retained the fragrance of violets that Lady Blackwold made liberal use of, and Hannah smiled as the scent tickled her nose.

She'd been extraordinarily fortunate to have escaped drowning and have the dowager's carriage stop for her. She couldn't imagine what might have happened to her if Beamish had simply driven past her, or if she'd taken just a few minutes longer to climb the cliff and had missed them altogether.

One of the wreckers had already been on the cliff—near enough to see her.

A sudden movement caught her attention. She peered into the darkness and pulled her shawls more tightly around her shoulders, suddenly feeling vulnerable in the darkness, even though she could clearly see the dowager sitting in her wing chair in front of the fire through the terrace doors.

Her mind whirled to the men who had been working on the beach all day, and from them to the wreckers.

No, they wouldn't come this close to Blackrock Manor, would they? She tried to shake off the feeling, but she couldn't. The golden glow from the room behind her illuminated her back, making her clearly visible to anyone who happened to be roaming through the winter garden.

"Is anyone there?" she called with a quick glance over her shoulder.

The dowager didn't move. Hannah's nervous voice hadn't disturbed her, at least.

"Miss Cowles?" Blackwold stepped up the shallow steps onto the terrace. The darkness clung to him, smudging his dark hair and blending into the dark fabric of his evening jacket.

"Is that you, Lord Blackwold?" She smiled in relief and moved back into the pool of light by the doors, hoping he would join her so that she could see him more clearly.

"Yes. What are you doing out here? A bit cool, is it not?"

"I wanted a breath of fresh air. I hadn't realized anyone else was out here."

As she hoped, he strode forward, stopping a bare yard from her. The flickering light coming through the doors showed that his carefully brushed hair had escaped the imposed order and with wild abandon curled in shaggy tufts over his ears. One thick lock hung over his brow, nearly obscuring his left eye. She longed to reach out and push the hair back in place and run her hands through the soft, brown waves. Helpless to control it, she took a step closer and felt her smile widen tenderly, her breath catching oddly as her heart thudded within her chest.

The starched, white neckcloth had come undone and hung down on either side of his open collar, exposing the strong column of his throat. His jacket was completely unbuttoned and only the two lowest buttons on his waistcoat remained chastely closed. He was so rumpled... And so dear because of it.

She leaned closer, unable to resist drinking in the fresh scent of the sea air combined with the heady, warm fragrance of his skin and the bay scent of the hair tonic his valet had used to attempt to bring order to his hair.

His eyes, though lost in shadows, seemed to gaze first into hers before dropping to her mouth.

She caught her breath and pulled her lower lip between her teeth, staring at his bare neck and broad shoulders. She moved another inch, wanting to feel the warmth and strength of him.

Reaching out one hand, he brushed his warm fingertips over her cheek and flicked aside one of her curls. His gaze intensified, focused on her mouth before his lips curved into a grin.

He touched the tip of her nose with his index finger. "Your nose is red, Miss Cowles. It's cold out here."

"Too cold," she said abruptly, stepping back. What had she been thinking?

Hands holding the edges of her shawl tightly, she strode to the terrace door, threw it open, and stepped into the warmth without glancing back to see if Blackwold was following her. She rubbed the tip of her nose with the back of her hand before she realized that she was most likely only making it a darker crimson.

He was laughing at her, she just knew it. And she was furious with herself for her previous, unaccountable desire to melt into his arms.

Red nose, indeed! Despite her irritation, though, she had to bite the insides of her cheeks to keep from laughing as she handed Lady Blackwold her borrowed cashmere shawl.

If Lady Blackwold had known what lay in Hannah's heart, she'd throw her out of the manor forthwith.

Chapter Seven

Grinning, Blackwold watched an indignant Miss Cowles return to the house.

She confused him, and he didn't particularly care for the feeling, having rarely felt it before.

On the one hand, he was suspicious of her and her motives in attaching herself to his grandmother. Another woman had done that two years ago, and before he'd realized what was happening and could take action, the dowager had unwisely invested most of her money in some scheme, only to see both her funds and the woman disappear into the night.

He was not going to see that happen again. While his grandmother rarely complained, it was obvious to the most lack-witted observer that she sorely missed her independence. The allowance he granted her, while generous, was clearly insufficient from her perspective and prevented her from spending money on any frippery that caught her attention. It galled her, particularly when he noticed and tried to make up for any deficit by purchasing whatever had caught her eye and presenting it to her.

She didn't want gifts—she wanted her independence.

He sighed and stared out at the darkness shrouding the garden, for the thousandth time going over what he knew about Miss Cowles.

There were a great many entries on the minus side of the ledger, to be sure. First was her arrival with a wealth of jewels in a plain linen pocket. Wealthy women didn't keep their precious baubles in pockets; they kept them safely locked away in velvet-lined boxes. Pockets were for bottles of smelling salts, handkerchiefs, small sewing kits, and other ridiculous items that ladies felt were important enough to carry around with them in a pocket tied around their waist under their skirts. And the pocket itself was not one of the extravagantly embroidered ones women like his grandmother carried. Miss Cowles's pocket was plain linen; the sort a less well-to-do woman might carry.

If the ship were sinking, tossed by the high winds and waves of a storm, one would think that Miss Cowles would be more concerned about her own life than her jewels. Even so, why would she not just grab the wooden box in which they surely belonged? Why take the time to put them in a pocket, unless she were actually hiding them under her skirts, hoping to steal them while the real Miss Cowles was distracted by the gale?

Which made him think of the companion of whom Miss Cowles spoke. Mrs. Lawrence. He hadn't missed her emotional response to the keepsake box they'd found on the beach, one which apparently belonged to Mrs. Lawrence. Would Miss Cowles really want a handful of letters written to another woman? Even if she were excessively attached to Mrs. Lawrence, the correspondence would surely have no meaning for her, no sentiment attached to them.

So, was Miss Cowles actually Mrs. Lawrence, pretending to be a wealthy heiress in hopes of gaining Miss Cowles's fortune? She seemed a trifle young for that, but one never knew.

Lastly, he remembered seeing a worried frown on Miss Cowles face, that often darkened her blue eyes with dread when she glanced at him. She had no reason to fear him if she were Miss Cowles, as she claimed. However, she knew that he mistrusted her claims, and as a result, she appeared to be frightened. Irritation he could understand. It would annoy him if those around him claimed he wasn't Lord Blackwold, but he wouldn't be afraid.

No. Fear indicated something else. Most likely, her anxiety rested upon the possibility that he might prove that she was not who, or what, she claimed to be.

Pacing across the terrace, he raked a hand through his hair. Despite the list of minuses, he *liked* her. She wasn't some shy, retiring female who was afraid to lift her gaze from the dusty floor, and she had a lively sense of humor. She clearly liked his grandmother, despite the dowager's often trenchant remarks, and was kind to her.

A smile flickered over his mouth. Miss Cowles was the first woman in a long time—actually, the first woman, ever—to grasp his odd sense of humor, and that was definitely something to go into the plus column. In fact, over the course of the day, he'd found himself seeking her out and making small jokes—very small ones—just to see the answering gleam of amusement in her blue eyes. Every time a small snort escaped her as she bent over her sewing, trying to suppress her laughter, he felt his mood soar like a gull on an ocean breeze.

Even after only knowing her for less than two days, he found himself glancing around when he entered a room, searching for the soft gleam of her fair hair and dancing eyes.

She seemed so honest, so open—even trusting. How could such a woman be an adventuress? She had none of the secretiveness he'd noticed in the woman who'd hurt his grandmother.

Except there was that fear he'd seen a few times in her eyes.

There were no easy answers, although he did wonder what she had in her trunk that could prove her claims so completely. Regardless, his main purpose now had to be to protect his grandmother. Miss Cowles—or Mrs. Lawrence—was really no concern of his, and he would soon be too busy to worry overmuch about her.

A cold knot settled in his stomach. He frowned and then moved toward the terrace doors. The night air was damp and getting colder by the minute, and he couldn't stay in the garden forever.

Standing outside was simply a moment of freedom, one of the few he could still enjoy. Such moments would become increasingly rare, all too soon. The trip to London would mark the end to his bachelor days, if everything went as planned, and why should it not?

The lawyers were already working on the legal documents that would tie Blackwold to a woman he'd met fewer than a half-dozen times. The arrangement had been planned by his father before he died—it was a good match for both of them.

Lady Alice was the daughter of an earl and would bring with her a dowry of fifty-thousand pounds. She was young and pretty, and he frankly didn't find her the least bit interesting. She'd seemed a cheerless sort the few times he'd met her, but perhaps that was simply politeness and a certain shyness.

Curious, though. He realized she had blonde hair and blue eyes very similar to Miss Cowles, but Lady Alice seemed almost colorless in comparison. Her gaze was a pale, chilly blue that seemed unable to grasp a great deal of what she observed, vastly unlike the deep rich blue of Miss Cowles's laughing eyes that were pleased and extremely observant a great deal of the time.

The metal doorknob felt icy under his palm, and he yanked the door open quickly. A rush of warm air brushed over him as he stepped inside.

The women were seated in front of the fire, Miss Cowles leaning toward his grandmother. Her long neck and the curve of her shoulders glowed golden from the firelight, and her silken gown shimmered pink with soft yellow highlights.

Laughing, the dowager shook her head at some comment made by Miss Cowles. She reached forward to give Miss Cowles's wrist a playful slap. Miss Cowles murmured something he couldn't hear and sat back. Although her back was to him, he could imagine a warm smile on her mouth.

He shook his head, brushing away such thoughts.

Nonetheless, he couldn't help but wonder, would his grandmother get along with Lady Alice so well? They seemed so unalike, at least on the surface. His grandmother was outspoken and quick to open her heart, covering her softness with the sharp thrusts of the verbal duels she enjoyed. Her moods were mercurial and had grown more so as she aged.

Lady Alice had struck him as a woman who had been petted and cosseted, and as a result, was woefully incapable of engaging in the type of witty conversation his grandmother adored. He could not imagine the two rubbing along together in one house.

His long fingers played with one of the buttons on his waistcoat, unconsciously unbuttoning it. He took a deep breath. Lady Alice was not the sort of woman who attracted him, but his father had wanted the match. It would serve both families well, and Blackwold had been well tutored to do his duty.

Marriage was a duty and a necessary evil that had nothing to do with emotions. While Lady Alice seemed a trifle insipid, he'd been reminded enough times to hear the words in his sleep: she would reflect well upon him. She would never create a scene, never do anything a lady should not do. The perfect wife.

Lady Alice would also never have fought wind and wave to survive a storm, or climb up to the road in a tattered evening dress with a plain linen pocket full of jewelry. Her pockets would undoubtedly be embroidered with silk, and would never contain anything except a small sewing kit, smelling salts, and a lace-edged handkerchief. His mouth quirked, his gaze resting on Miss Cowles's long, elegant neck.

Lady Alice would undoubtedly have done the right thing and died like a proper English lady.

Chuckling to himself, he stepped into the pool of light, watching Miss Cowles. She lifted her head immediately and straightened, her gaze fluttering from his grandmother to his face.

The wavering light cast sharp shadows around her eyes and under her cheekbones. She shivered and covered the involuntary movement by drawing her light shawl closer. The lamp on a small, square table at her elbow highlighted the fairness of her skin. His grin slowly changed into a frown.

She was more than fair—she was pallid, and the shadows under her eyes weren't just the effect of the uneven glow from the fire. The rigid set of her body and face spoke of someone who was desperately holding herself together, trying not to be ill.

It was damp outside—she'd been a fool to go out there and risk a chill after her experiences two nights prior.

He faced his grandmother. "It's late, Grandmother. Time to retire."

She stared past his shoulder at the ornate clock on the mantel. Her mouth worked for a few seconds, her gray brows drawn together over her nose. "It is barely half past nine, Blackwold."

"Nonetheless, I'm off to bed," he replied cheerfully. He stretched and then held a fist in front of his mouth as he yawned. "You ladies may be prepared to sit up all night, but I assure you, I'm not."

Miss Cowles stood as he spoke. She swayed and then gripped the back of her chair, her lips compressed into a thin line. For a moment, she remained silent, the muscles in her neck working as she swallowed. "Will you excuse me, Lady Blackwold?" she said in a soft voice.

"Well, I am not so paltry and weak that I wish to retire before ten!" the dowager stated. She wriggled deeper into her chair and fixed her gaze on the fire. "When I was your age, I would dance all night and think nothing of it."

"Yes, but not the second evening after being washed ashore in a gale," he replied dryly. He bent and kissed his grandmother's wrinkled cheek.

She bit her lips to keep from smiling, and he gave her clasped hands a squeeze before he straightened. "Well, nonetheless, I will be the good host and remain here. Henry is bound to want some company—he is not as delicate as some I could mention."

"Ah, yes, Henry. I neglected to give you his regards, Grandmother. He was feeling fatigued and retired an hour ago," he replied.

He'd been surprised, himself, when Henry elected to go straight to his bedchamber after dinner, when he'd made it so clear earlier that he was fascinated by their young guest.

But perhaps Miss Cowles wasn't the only one feeling unwell.

"So, you all plan to desert me!" the dowager exclaimed.

"Perhaps I could..." Miss Cowles voice drifted off and the muscles in her neck and jaw clenched as she pressed her lips together.

"No. You could not." Blackwold gripped her elbow and turned her toward the door. "Goodnight, Grandmother. Sleep well."

"Yes, yes." She waved them away.

"Goodnight," Miss Cowles murmured.

Her meek compliance as he led her through the door convinced him that she was mere minutes away from collapse. But she was not the sort of woman to complain or even admit her weakness. There was no point in asking her if she were well, or needed assistance.

So, he guided her to her bedchamber, rang for Mary, and left Miss Cowles standing in the middle of her room, her gaze fixed a little too grimly on the washbasin.

Chapter Eight

"You're awake!" an appallingly chipper voice exclaimed.

Hannah's eyelids felt sticky as she turned her aching head. Her stomach rumbled, hollow and sore, and she had a terrible taste in her mouth, but at least her joints no longer ached with fever. She glanced around, struggling to sit up, and was surprised at how weak and shaky she felt.

"Who?" Hannah glanced in the direction of the voice.

A young woman leaned closer. Soft brown curls framed a lovely, dimpled face, and her large brown eyes twinkled with bouncy good humor. "I've been waiting *ages* for you to awaken! You've been sick for *days*!"

"Days?" Hannah repeated, finally sliding up enough to partially sit up against her pillows. She glanced around the room, feeling lost and confused.

"Yes—you've been *frightfully* ill! Blackwold wouldn't even allow Grandmother to visit you for fear you would make her ill, too. The only person who is even permitted inside your room is Mary." Eyes shining with glee, she leaned forward and gripped Hannah's wrist. "But I came in this morning, anyway. I wanted to see the infamous Miss Cowles from Boston—is it true that you were fighting off a man at the top of the cliffs when Beamish halted the coach and rescued you?"

"Fighting off a man?" Hannah repeated. Her throat and mouth burned—she desperately wanted a glass of water. Who was this extraordinary young woman anyway, and what was she doing in her bedroom?

The girl nodded, her brown curls bobbing around her plump cheeks. "Is it really true?" She clasped her hands together. "How exciting! Was he a *wrecker*?"

"A wrecker?" Hannah repeated, the room spinning around her. Maybe it was just her illness that made her mishear what the girl had said.

The brunette nodded, her curls bouncing around her face. "Was he trying to *ravish* you? Were you frightened? Was it horrible?"

"No! That is, there was no wrecker. Where did you hear that dreadful tale?"

The brunette reached out and pressed her hand on Hannah's arm, giving her a warmly sympathetic look. "You needn't be afraid of what I might think—I'm convinced you were quite brave. I don't care if you *are* no better than you should be." She covered her mouth with one hand as she giggled. "That sounds so silly—don't you agree? But how *exciting!* Did you push him over the cliff when he accosted you? I believe I would have, unless you *wanted* him to accost you, of course. Was he very handsome? If not, it was a good thing that Grandmother came along when she did, was it not?"

"No! Yes! That is, I'm grateful to your grandmother, of course, but there was no wrecker—I didn't push anyone over the cliff. I was alone. There was no wrecker, truly. Where did you hear that story?"

"Why, *everyone* in the village is talking about it. My uncle said it was such a pity, too, that you failed to perish when the *Orion* sank, as you might prove to be yet another bad influence for Grandmother, and she does *not* need any more *bad* influences."

Dazed by the flood of gossip, Hannah tried to swallow. Her throat burned. She glanced at her bedside table. "Is there any water?"

"Oh, yes!" The girl leapt out of her chair, laughing. "I am so sorry." She dashed over to a tall chest of drawers and picked up a white china pitcher. Water sloshed into a teacup, and Hannah winced as it slurped over the edge onto the wooden surface of the chest. But the girl didn't seem to notice or care. Carrying the cup, she returned to Hannah and carefully placed it in her hands. "There." She giggled and pressed her fingers over her mouth. "Sorry. I'm such a chatterbox—Blackwold says I'd talk the ears off a donkey, but you don't mind, do you? You look so nice, and I feel as if we already know each other, even though we've never been introduced. Oh!" She laughed. "You must be wondering who I am—but I assure you I'm not the ninny or terrible chatterbox Blackwold insists I am."

"Really? That *is* good to hear." Hannah drained the cup. Although the water was tepid at best, it tasted sweet to her parched tongue.

"I'm Georgina Hodges—but I hope you will call me Gina. I despise the name *Georgie*—I don't know why. George is such a kingly name, though, and I'm not at all kingly. And Gina is so much nicer, don't you agree?"

"Yes," Hannah agreed weakly.

Gina snatched the cup out of her hand, splashed some more water into it, and handed it back to Hannah with a wide grin.

"Thank you," Hannah said. "And I'm Hannah, though I suspect you already know that."

So, this was the grandchild the dowager was preparing to present to Society. Hannah nodded and smiled as the girl continued to speak, unable to resist the younger girl's enthusiasm. Gina couldn't have been more than eighteen years old, and her vivacity and the sparkle in her eyes made it hard to do anything except grin back.

She immediately liked her—she couldn't believe that anyone would *not* like her, in fact. But more than that, Hannah had the warming sense that she'd found a real friend.

"Oh, yes. And you *are* nice, no matter what they are saying in the village."

Gina's flood of words washed back over Hannah, and she eyed the girl. "You said your *uncle* had told you that I was with a man?"

"Oh, yes." Gina nodded vigorously. "Uncle Carter. He's the vicar in the village—Pencroft—and one of the *steady* Hodges, like Cousin Henry. Very precise, but so very handsome. Cousin Henry is quite the paragon of fashion, don't you agree?"

"Yes—"

"And he is such a gentleman. He never forgets my birthday. Every year he gives me a yellow silk ribbon—my favorite color—and, of course, something else nice. Last year he gave me a lovely box of chocolate confections, which I just adored! My father always forgets, but Cousin Henry never fails me. He really is the kindest one of us. As opposed to the *mad* Hodges." She frowned. "My father says I'm one of the mad Hodges, just like Blackwold, but I disagree because even *I* fail to understand Blackwold, and I would understand him if I were mad as well, wouldn't I?"

"Well—"

"He is always making these peculiar *remarks,* and frankly, they either prove that he is indeed quite mad, or he doesn't know what he is saying, because they don't make the least sense. Or they are terribly offensive, which I don't think he intends to be. If he weren't a marquess, I'm convinced the family would lock him in the cellars, along with the brandy."

A twinge of sadness at Gina's sad view of her cousin made Hannah let out a long breath.

So even Blackwold's little cousin didn't understand him, or his wry sense of humor. How frustrating it must be for him.

Slowly, a smile played at her mouth. Warmth spread through her at the sense of a shared secret with the misunderstood marquess. His sense of humor touched an answering chord in her, one she never knew existed.

"He does have a very subtle sense of humor," Hannah said.

"Subtle? Don't tell me that he makes sense to you!" Gina exclaimed, her eyes widening.

"I must be mad, too," Hannah said, biting the inside of her mouth to keep from laughing.

"Oh, you are teasing me—honestly—you must be feeling better to say such a thing."

"Yes, I do feel better." Hannah's smile slowly changed into a confused frown. "But your uncle, why would he think I was wrestling with a man when I was not doing any such a thing?"

"I expect he heard the gossip, though you'd have thought that the storm and wreck of the *Orion* would have been a rich enough mine of gossip without talking about you, too." She shrugged. "I suppose it is because you are from the United States of America." A wistful look passed over her face, and she chewed on her plump lower lip. "You are so fortunate to be able to travel."

"I suppose so." She certainly didn't *feel* fortunate. In fact, if she had her way, she'd find a nice snug home and never set out on another journey for the rest of her life. "But you are going to London soon, and that is a start."

"Yes." Gina's lack of enthusiasm was obvious in the drooping curve of her mouth. She smoothed her sprigged muslin skirts and picked at an invisible speck of dust. "Just to fling myself at some man's head."

"Maybe you will fall in love," Hannah replied wistfully. "And perhaps he will enjoy traveling. My father adored exploring the world and took us with him everywhere he went. You might find someone similar."

"Perhaps." Gina's expressive face suddenly grew cold, as if every warm emotion had drained away. She shrugged, her slender fingers now picking at the silk edge of the blanket covering Hannah. "But only if he has a title and meets with my grandmother's approval."

"If you fell in love, I'm sure she would approve."

Gina glanced away, her face a mask emptied of emotion.

Icy dismay settled in the hollow of Hannah's admittedly empty stomach. Surely, the dowager wouldn't force Gina to marry someone she didn't love, merely for the sake of a title?

Unfortunately, she was all too aware that for many women, marriage was a business decision. Emotions had nothing to do with the matter, and one was fortunate, indeed, if any affection at all grew within the bonds of matrimony.

Hannah's father may have dragged them hither and yon until she was so footsore and weary that she could barely stand the thought of looking at another map, or climbing into another carriage, but she knew in the depths of her heart that he would never expect her to marry someone she did not love. He had married his childhood sweetheart, a woman as enamored of traveling as he was, and he'd never appeared to regret it, despite the occasional hushed argument.

He'd never gotten over her death, either, but at least he'd had nineteen glorious years with a woman he loved. And he hadn't suffered his final loneliness very long. He'd passed away only a few years later.

The silence stretched uncomfortably around them. Hannah shifted in her bed, weak and tired, despite having been in bed for hours, if not days. She looked at Gina, searching for something that would bring back the dimpled smile to her round face.

As she opened her mouth to speak, the door creaked. Mary entered sideways, carrying a wooden tray draped with white linen.

Gina leapt to her feet, her round cheeks flushed with guilt.

The movement caught Mary's attention, and a frown creased the maid's forehead. "Miss Hodges! You should not be in here—the dowager Lady Blackwold specifically said that you should not risk your health in this careless manner!"

Gina giggled and flashed a bright-eyed glance at Hannah. "You know very well, dear Mary, that it was *you* who insisted that no one visit Miss Cowles except you, you selfish creature! Grandmother has wanted to visit for *days,* and you positively *blockaded* the door. One would think you had a chest of gold hidden in here instead of one poor, sick woman."

Mouth open, Hannah's hands clenched the covers as she transferred her gaze to the maid, expecting the worst.

Instead of anger, a smile tugged at Mary's thin mouth. She sucked in her lips, clearly trying not to grin as she shook her head. "It were for your own good, Miss Hodges, as well you know." She flicked a sheepish glance at Hannah. "And for my patient's sake. You chatter worse than a greenfinch, and Miss Cowles needs her rest."

"Yes, but she's rested for days now, and is dying for company." Gina turned to look at Hannah. "Are you not?"

Hannah nodded and struggled to swing her legs out of bed, though they seemed to be tangled in the heavy covers.

"What are you about?" Mary shrieked, rushing in to set the tray on top of the dresser next to the door. "See what you have done, Miss Hodges!" She ran over to the bed and grabbed Hannah's shoulders, pushing her back into the pillows. "Stay where you are—you cannot rise yet, Miss! Whatever be you thinking?"

"I'm sorry." Hannah sank back, too weak to push against Mary's strong grip. "However, I dislike eating in bed." Crumbs always resulted, and ants soon followed. She stifled a shudder.

"Dislike or not, you shall do so!" Mary replied sharply.

Gina laughed and moved toward the door. "I will leave you to your breakfast."

"But—"

"I'll return this afternoon," Gina said. "I promise."

Mary's head swiveled in her direction, her brows creasing. "You will not—"

"I will, *too!* With a *book!*" Gina's reply sounded like a dreadful threat.

Mary's lips trembled again. She pressed them together and picked up the tray from the dresser. "If you become too ill to go to London, don't blame me. I cannot be expected to do more than I've done, now can I?"

"No, indeed," Gina said, her eyes twinkling. "You've done everything humanly possible to keep Miss Cowles imprisoned. I'm sure no one can blame you in the least, or accuse you of excessive amiability." With that, she slipped through the door and closed it before Mary could reply.

Half-fearing that the maid would unleash her frustration upon her, Hannah watched Mary as she brought the tray to the bed and set it carefully upon her knees. The warm scent of beef broth rose as the maid lifted off the linen napkin covering the dishes. Or dish.

Despite the large size of the tray, the only thing on it was a bowl of clear beef broth.

Mary stepped back and folded her hands at her waist, her gaze fixed on Hannah's face.

Oh, no. I'm in for it now.

"Finish your broth, now, like a good girl, and perhaps you may have a piece of dry toast for your tea," Mary said. She stared at Hannah and then bent down, her hand hovering over the spoon. "Let me help you."

"No—no, thank you." Hannah picked up the spoon and plunged it into the bowl. The broth was rich and savory, with a faint but unmistakable hint of delicious rosemary, but a couple of spoonfuls only made her aware of how hungry she really was.

"You mustn't let Miss Hodges disturb you." Mary smoothed the covers and tucked them securely under the edges of the mattress, effectively trapping Hannah in bed.

She didn't think she could so much as move a leg, however, at least the maid didn't appear angry. In fact, she had a curiously tender look on her face as she turned to straighten the already clean room.

"I enjoyed her visit," Hannah said between spoonfuls. "How long was I ill?"

"Four days, Miss. The doctor came and bled you twice—there weren't nothing else to be done." Instead of her usual, dour expression, Mary's gray eyes were filled with sympathy as she watched Hannah finish her broth. "Makes your arms ache, though, don't it? Never liked being bled, myself."

"No. And you are right, my left arm is very sore."

"Then don't use it—no need for now." She lifted the tray from Hannah's lap before Hannah could do more than drop her spoon next to her bowl. "You just rest and let me take care of you—you'll be up in no time."

"Thank you, Mary." Hannah felt overwhelmed, and perhaps it was the lingering effect of her illness, but warm tears stung her eyes. She blinked and busied herself with pulling the covers up.

Clearly, Mary needed to feel that she was wanted— perhaps Hannah had been too independent before to earn her friendship. Whatever the reason, the maid seemed inclined to treat her now like one of her own children— requiring cosseting and attention.

"Now you go back to sleep. No reason to stir."

"Yes," Hannah answered drowsily. Though her stomach was still tender and uneasy, she was by no means full. However, she felt content. The broth had sent warmth and an increasing lassitude through her limbs.

Mary smiled and nodded before she turned. The door creaked softly as she slipped away with the tray, leaving Hannah to fall into a deep slumber.

Chapter Nine

Driven by all-too-well-known insomnia, Blackwold glanced up and down the corridor and eased open the door. The moonlight streaming through the window revealed Miss Cowles's sleeping form, curled up under heavy covers. He gently closed the door behind him and moved over to the bed.

The maid had braided Miss Cowles's fair hair, but soft, pale strands around her face had escaped and lay over her cheek, moving with each soft breath. Even gilded by the silvery light, he recognized signs of her illness in the deep circles beneath the flutter of her lashes and the hollows under her cheekbones.

He touched her wrist lightly.

Her eyelids sprang open immediately. "Who is there? What is it?"

"Quietly, Miss Cowles," he replied.

"Lord Blackwold!" She glanced around and struggled to sit up, but he placed a heavy hand on her shoulder.

"Peace. Don't get up on my account."

"Don't get up on *your* account!" She brushed him off and sat up, plumping the pillows behind her to support her back. "What are you doing in here?" She looked around again. "What time is it?"

"It is a little past three in the morning—the most honest time of the day."

"Hardly the day. And I fail to see how the middle of the night is any more honest than any other hour."

He picked up a ladder-backed chair and brought it closer to the bed. Taking a seat, he grinned. "People seem more inclined to share their honest opinions in the dark. Or when sleepy. Don't you find it so?"

"Since I'm usually in bed at this hour—"

"Exactly."

She held her hand up in front of her mouth to hide her laugh, but her soft snort betrayed her. "What are you doing here at three in the morning?"

"You might consider speaking more softly, Miss Cowles. If you don't wish for more company."

"Mary will be furious with you if she finds out. I'm supposed to be resting." The moonlight revealed the flash of her eyes as she gave him a sidelong glance. She bit her lower lip.

"So, you are." He hooked one arm over the back of his chair and lounged back. "I couldn't sleep, and I thought you might be suffering from the same restlessness." He gestured to the window. "Full moon."

"I'm suffering from no such thing, as you very well know, since you decided to awaken me at this wretched hour." She shifted against her pillows and arranged the covers with nervous hands. "Surely, you didn't come in here just to annoy me." She stifled a yawn. "Unlike you, I really do not have any difficulties sleeping."

He caught her left wrist and held it gently, his fingers finding her pulse. It beat firmly, though perhaps a bit fast. "Apparently not." He smiled, and when she tried to withdraw her hand, he tightened his grip. "So. I understand you met my cousin, Georgina."

"Yes. She's a delightful girl."

"Unlike the rest of the Hodges?"

"Oh, are there other girls in your family?" Her overly sweet reply held distinct tones of sarcasm.

His grin widened. "I'm glad you like her—she was enormously impressed by you."

"Is that what this is about? You think it is inappropriate for me to associate with such an innocent and impressionable young woman?"

"Your voice, Miss Cowles. Do modulate your tones, or you really will awaken the dragon."

"I can assure you that my friendship with Gina will do her no harm," Miss Cowles whispered with sibilant ferocity.

"No. If I were to be concerned about either of you, it would not be my cousin. Particularly when you are in this weakened state."

"I am not *weak*!"

His brows rose. "Truly? Mary insists that you have no more strength than a kitten and will be confined to your room for at least another two days. Perhaps more."

"I will *not*!" She replied coldly. Her wrist jerked in his grasp, but her pulse remained firm and steady. "I intend to get up tomorrow morning—that is, assuming that I will be allowed to sleep tonight, which doesn't seem at all likely."

"That moonlight is damned intrusive, is it not?" He shook his head. "You should have pulled your curtains closed if it bothers you so much."

He was rewarded with another stifled snort and a tug from the hand he held. "Can't you just go away and get drunk like a decent British lord? Why must you bother me?"

"No reason, except a touch of curiosity." He shifted his fingers over the smooth skin of her wrist to find the flutter of her pulse again. "Why are you frightened of me, Miss Cowles? What did you see the night the *Orion* sank?"

Her pulse kicked up, throbbing rapidly under his fingertips. She tried to pull her arm away, but he refused to allow it. Her face was masklike in the moonlight, her cheekbones sharply defined and her eyes sunken in hollows. It was cruel of him to press her so when she'd been ill and was at her weakest, but that was also the time when she was at her most vulnerable. If she was going to reveal the truth, it would be now, when she was muzzy-headed from sleep and shaky from sickness.

"I told you—I saw nothing. Just the storm. I didn't have time to observe anything except jagged rocks, waves, and a treacherous path through them to the shore." She pressed her lips together.

"What do you fear?"

"I fear nothing!"

"And yet the pounding of your heart says otherwise."

"Perhaps I simply fear that you will take advantage of me, and perhaps I am right to fear that, since here you are, in my room at three in the morning, for no reason except an inability to sleep."

Her words stung, but he didn't move or release her. In his same soft, even voice, he said, "If that is what you fear, then set your mind at rest."

"Because you don't find me attractive enough to molest?" Her mouth twisted.

"Do you *want* me to ravish you?" He grinned wolfishly.

She glanced down at the covers and smoothed them over her lap with her free hand. "I just want you to let me rest."

"And I will—once you answer my questions. What exactly did you see, Miss Cowles?"

"Hannah." She sighed heavily, her right hand restlessly moving over the covers to pick at the seams. "You might as well call me Hannah."

"Very well, Hannah. What did you see?"

"Why do you insist I saw something? I'd be dead if I saw them, would I not?" She pressed her lips together, then her eyes widened. Her hand flew up to press against her mouth.

"As I thought." He nodded. "You did see the wreckers— and you saw what they did." His voice was harsh, and he modulated his tones with difficulty. "And you thought I was one of them."

"I saw you!"

Now that was interesting. He studied her pale face, trying to read her thoughts from her eyes and frowning mouth, but the shadows guarded her expression too well. "You saw a man you thought was I. Did you see his face?"

Mouth pressed into a firm line again, she shook her head. Beneath his fingertips, the racing of her pulse was slowly returning to normal.

"I see." He considered this for a moment before nodding. He lifted his right hand. The griffin ring gleamed dully in the silvery light from the window, the diamond eyes dark. "You saw a ring, then. This ring?"

"The head of an animal with wings. Yes. A griffin with jeweled eyes." She bit off the words, her gaze focused on her lap. "Or perhaps I only thought I saw it. How do I know? It was dark, and I was fighting the storm to stay alive."

"But there were lanterns. There are always lanterns when they want to draw a ship in to shore."

"I don't know anything. The storm—I hardly know what I saw." Her mouth trembled, and she bit her lower lip again. "I won't tell anyone. Just leave me in peace."

"I have no intention of harming you. But do try to act a little less terrified when I enter the room. It's demoralizing."

A sob, half tears and half laughter, escaped her before she once again covered her mouth with her hand. He released her left wrist, and she rubbed it vigorously before pulling the covers even higher. "And I told you—I am not afraid of you."

"If you saw this ring then you ought to be," he commented. "But you didn't see the face that went with it?"

She shook her head.

"Did you see the color of the eyes?"

"No. I couldn't see your—his—face." Her voice shook.

"The eyes of the griffin?"

"No."

"But you saw enough to be frightened."

Another soft cry caught in her throat.

"And you are tired." He relented, feeling cruel for having forced her into a confession, even one as useless as hers proved to be. He ran a hand through his hair. "I wish you had seen his face."

"Well, I don't! I'm glad I didn't see his face."

"Ignorance will not keep you safe, Hannah. Quite the reverse." He lifted his right fist and tilted it to catch the pale light with his ring. "There are four rings. Who will you trust?"

"I don't know, though there is one thing I do know. I can trust that you will not let me sleep, and you will annoy me to your utmost, even though you don't find me attractive enough to bother ravishing. Even when you are alone with me in my room at three in the morning."

"You sound exceedingly displeased about it, too." A smile played over his mouth as he studied her. He rose slowly and bent over the bed, bracing himself with one arm resting on the headboard and the other stretched over her lap, his fist planted on the covers next to her hip.

"What are you doing?" she asked breathlessly. Her right hand pressed against her chest while her left clutched the silk edge of her blanket.

He stared into her eyes, wide and dark in the moonlight. The thick plaits of her pale hair framed her long neck, and as he watched, the tip of her tongue brushed over her lower lip. She smelled of lavender, rosemary, and honey, and her skin appeared silvery in the light from the window.

He pressed his lips against the smooth, warm skin of her forehead. The lace of her nightcap brushed his nose, tickling it with the scent of clean soap. The muscles in his arms tightened briefly before he straightened.

"Good night, Hannah. Sleep well." He moved toward the door.

Silence answered him. When he turned to look at her from the doorway, she was staring at him, her lips slightly parted.

He grinned back, wishing he could see the blush he knew must be covering her cheeks, but the moonlight only painted her in shades of silver and black. When she frowned, he stepped into the hallway and shut the door behind him.

A little knowledge was a dangerous thing. Why the devil had he ridden out in response to Farley, that idiot of a Customs Officer, on the one night that the wreckers decided to lure a ship in on Blackrock's doorstep? If he had been there...

All he could do now was try to keep her safe and puzzle out which of his relatives was encouraging the villagers to commit murder.

Chapter Ten

Hannah repeatedly rearranged her pillows and covers, feeling at once too flushed and too cold.

She could still feel Blackwold's warm lips pressed against her forehead, and she couldn't rid herself of the disappointment that he hadn't pressed that light kiss on her mouth, instead. Unforgivably, she'd even lifted her chin when he leaned over her, his white shirt gaping open at the neck and the scent of bay soap and warm skin filling the space between them. Her heart had pounded in her chest as she waited, breathing in his fragrance, longing to reach up and brush that ridiculous lock of shaggy brown hair out of his eyes.

She'd wanted him to kiss her, desperately. Wantonly.

Perhaps she was the one who was so mad that she ought to be locked up in the cellars along with the brandy, as Gina remarked about Blackwold.

It took a long time for her pulse to settle back to its regular calm beat and even longer for drowsiness to return and pull her back to sleep.

Dawn had barely tinted the sky a crystalline peach when her door creaked again. A white-capped head peered through the gap.

"Are you awake?" Gina whispered.

Hannah sat up with a smile. "Yes. And I'm impatient to leave this room."

"Oh, good!" Gina entered, and after a quick glance down the hallway, she closed the door behind her. "Ever since Papa left yesterday, I have been bored to tears. I'm so glad you are feeling better."

Before Hannah could reply, the door opened again. Her hand pressed against her chest as her pulse leapt in anticipation that Blackwold had been gripped by the same impulse as Gina had experienced to visit Hannah at dawn.

A tray appeared and then Mary. She glanced at Hannah and then Gina, her stern expression softening until she almost appeared to smile. "Miss Hodges—you are up early."

"Yes, I am." Gina stepped over to the maid, gave her a quick kiss on the cheek, and took the tray away from her. "Here you are, Hannah. I suppose we must do without you at breakfast, but I absolutely insist that you join me thereafter for a walk. Perhaps we can venture into Pencroft? We can have tea at Uncle Carter's." She glanced uneasily at Mary and amended her plans. "If you feel strong enough." Her brown eyes sparkled with anticipation mixed with hesitancy as she looked from Hannah to Mary and back.

Grinning, Hannah nodded and accepted the tray, balancing it on her lap. A walk in the fresh air was just the thing she needed to clear her mind, and she wasn't so hard-hearted that she would deny Gina the treat she clearly wanted.

To be completely honest, she was also curious to see Pencroft.

And she couldn't forget that Carter Hodges also had a griffin ring, although since he was a vicar, it seemed highly unlikely that he would order the death of anyone, let alone Officer Trent. She frowned, considering Gina's comment that her father had already left. He also had a ring, and he was a captain. What if he'd left because he feared that Hannah may have seen him on the beach that dreadful night and might recognize him?

A shiver went down her back. *What a horrible thought.* She absolutely did not want Gina's father to be a cold-hearted murderer. But once the idea had occurred to her, it was difficult to dismiss.

When she glanced up, both Mary and Gina were eyeing her, Gina with lifted brows and a hopeful expression on her face, and Mary with a very thoughtful look furrowing her brow.

"You ain't strong yet," Mary interjected, clasping her work-worn hands together against the snowy white apron she wore over her dark dress. "It's near a mile or more to Pencroft."

"Yes, but the sun is out, and we shall go ever so slowly," Gina said, turning to the maid and grasping her arm imploringly. "If she gets too tired, I'm sure Uncle Carter will bring us back in a cart."

"You know very well your uncle don't have no cart, Miss Hodges, him being a vicar and all." A smile lit her eyes and teased the corners of her mouth for a second before she forced her features into a more serious expression. "Poor as a church mouse."

Gina sighed, her grip on Mary's wrist tightening. "You know he can borrow one any time he wishes from the inn. He is not too poor to do *that*."

"Well, what I knows is that it's assuming a great deal to expect him to," Mary replied tartly. "Him being a vicar and all."

"If it comes to that, I can well afford to hire a gig." Gina smiled at Hannah. "Papa is very generous, and I haven't had the least chance to spend even *half* of what he provided me this month."

Mary snorted and shook her head.

But even Hannah could see that the maid was slowly coming around to agreement with Gina's impulsive idea, and she was relieved that Gina had undertaken the task to convince Mary instead of Hannah. If she'd insisted on going, she was fairly sure Mary would have resorted to removing all of Hannah's gowns so that she couldn't go out, even if she wished to do so.

"So, it is quite settled," Gina said, releasing her hold on Mary's arm. "I am going to dress. We can leave as soon as you are ready, Hannah."

"I'm looking forward to it." Hannah turned her attention to the contents of the tray. When she lifted the linen napkin covering it, she found a basket full of warm rolls, pots of butter and peach preserves, and even a soft-boiled egg in a fragile bone china eggcup. The yeasty fragrance of the rolls made her stomach gurgle with hunger.

She broke open a roll and watched a delicate puff of yeasty steam escape before she slathered both the butter and preserves on the tender, fresh bread. Her attention was completely absorbed by the delicious rolls, egg, and the sweet pot of hot chocolate, so she felt surprised when she glanced up to see that Mary had laid out a warm walking dress in rich blue and a heavy navy blue pelisse on the end of the bed.

"You'll want a shawl, as well," Mary stated as she picked up the tray. The empty dishes clattered beneath the wrinkled napkin. "The dowager'll give you her cashmere and a bonnet. I found them boots there—I'm sure they'll fit." The certainty in her statements revealed her long-time familiarity with the Hodges family, and her confidence in her position as a lady's maid.

"I'm sure they will," Hannah agreed meekly. She wasn't about to undo all the work Gina had accomplished in convincing Mary that Hannah was ready to walk to the village.

When she first stood, she had to grab the bedpost to keep from falling onto her face. Her legs trembled, and she had a light-headed, dizzy feeling, but the sensations soon diminished. She staggered over to the washbasin. The cold water had a bracing effect, enough so that she was grateful when she pulled on the warm clothing that Mary had set out for her. The maid soon returned with a heavy shawl over her arm and a bonnet swinging from her hand. She assisted her to dress, fussing and clicking her tongue, but she didn't try to persuade Hannah that it was too soon after her illness for such an outing.

After buttoning up the warm pelisse and arranging the shawl over her shoulders, Hannah thanked Mary and found her way downstairs as quickly as possible.

Sparkling laughter drifted through the library door near the foot of the stairs, revealing Gina's presence. Hannah's heart lifted. Smiling, she walked into the room.

Gina and the dowager were sitting cozily close to the fire, and Gina had one hand on Lady Blackwold's wrist as she leaned forward to speak to her. Both ladies were grinning and seemed to be sharing such a pleasant conversation that Hannah suffered a sharp pang. She felt like a rude intruder standing there, a foreigner at the manor on sufferance. She almost hated to interrupt them.

Before she could speak, Gina glanced up. Welcome flashed in her huge brown eyes and her dimples deepened as her grin widened. "Hannah! Are you ready to go to Pencroft?"

"Yes, if you still want to go." She caught the dowager's gaze. "I apologize for interrupting."

Lady Blackwold snorted and flicked her wrist to release Gina's grasp. "You look like a ghost from my past, pallid and standing there in my old pelisse and bonnet. But if you believe you are well enough to walk to the village, you have my blessing." She frowned and glanced around the room. "I haven't the least notion where Blackwold or Henry have gone." She sighed and shook her head. "However, I suppose a lack of male companionship will not stop two such modern young women from galloping across the landscape in any direction they wish."

Standing, Gina covered her mouth, but a merry giggle still escaped her. "I have Hannah and she has me for company, so we shall be quite proper, I assure you. And we will stop for tea at the vicarage, and *nothing* could be more proper than that."

Lady Blackwold snorted. "Well, there is no convincing you otherwise, I'm sure. So, I won't even try. Give my love to your uncle Carter and tell him it wouldn't be amiss for the vicar to perform his duty once in a while and visit his old, widowed mother. I daresay he has sufficient time to visit any number of ladies in the village to give them the benefit of his counsel and support, so he can find the time for me."

"But you *know* you don't need his counsel, dear Grandmother. Quite the reverse," Gina replied with a laugh. She bent and kissed the dowager on the cheek and gave her shoulder a squeeze. "But I shall tell him you are awaiting a visit from him. No doubt he will come immediately. Or nearly so." She looked at Hannah. "He may even bring us back and stay for supper."

"Or he will have some excuse, as he usually does," Lady Blackwold replied in a dry voice. She shook her head and waved them away. "No matter. Be gone, you two, and leave me be. Alone. Sitting here by the fire with no one to talk to." She let out a heavy sigh. "Not that it matters."

Frowning, Hannah stepped forward, but Gina caught her arm and shook her head, her eyes twinkling with mirth. "Never fear, Grandmother. You can always ring for Mary."

"That dour old woman? I'd sooner drink a pint of vinegar."

"She's at least thirty years younger than you, dearest Grandmother," Gina pointed out sweetly. "However, perhaps Blackwold is around somewhere. I'm sure he will be glad to keep you company. Well, we must be off." She yanked Hannah to the door and closed it behind them before her grandmother could reply.

In a matter of minutes, they'd stepped outdoors. The air was crisp and carried the unmistakable salt tang of the sea. The distant cry of gulls rang through the air, and Hannah caught the trim form of a tern pass overhead. She took a deep breath. As the fresh, clean air filled her lungs, it seemed to push all the remaining illness and weakness away.

Overhead, white fluffy clouds scudded across the crystal blue sky, and despite the sere, gray and black winter landscape, she felt a surge of happiness. Some green was rising through the ground, life anew sprouting, and it was good to be outside on such a glorious day.

Linking arms with Hannah, Gina set a moderate pace, chattering about inconsequential things, starting with the fine weather, the color of the sky and how it was just a few shades lighter than Hannah's eyes, the ribbons one might acquire in the village that might also match Hannah's blue eyes, and from there, various points of current fashion.

Hannah nodded contentedly, only half-listening. Fashion had never really interested her, although she did appreciate fine clothing. A gust of chilly wind trickled down the hollow of her neck, and she fastened the top button of her pelisse and pulled the thick shawl more closely around her. Walking kept her mostly warm, and the kid boots Mary had given her did fit fairly well, but the breeze was still a little raw and damp.

By the time they reached the village, Hannah's feet were dragging, and her limbs were shaking. Perhaps it was too soon to go on such a long walk. She slumped a little when Gina dragged her into a small shop on the busy main street of Pencroft.

Instead of the male shopkeeper she expected, a very plump woman greeted them with pleasure, her round face dimpling and her dark eyes sparkling, the image of a woman who enjoyed gossiping almost as much as selling her goods. "Miss Hodges! I heard you were here, visiting your grandmother, the Dowager Lady Blackwold. What an honor to see you in my little shop!"

"Yes, Mrs. Shaw." Gina pulled Hannah forward. "I brought my friend, Miss Cowles, lately from Boston. Miss Cowles, this is Mrs. Shaw, the owner of this lovely emporium."

Mrs. Shaw's smile disappeared for a moment. Her gaze hardened so briefly that Hannah wondered if she'd truly seen the narrowing of her eyes. Then, mindful of Gina's presence, Mrs. Shaw nodded. "An honor, I'm sure." Her face brightened, and she bent behind the counter where she stood and pulled out a wide box, which she set on the scarred wooden surface. "I got them ribbons I told you about last time you was here, Miss Hodges." She flicked open the lid and shoved it beneath the counter, all the while smiling at Gina.

"Oh! Do you have any yellow ones?" Gina stepped forward and bent over the box, sifting through the rainbow colors of silk ribbons.

"Yes." Mrs. Shaw laughed. "No need to tangle them into knots." She deftly began pulling out ribbons in all shades of yellow, from the palest to the richest golden color that turned almost orange in the sunlight. "There's any color you wish, Miss Hodges. I ordered them special, hoping you'd honor us with a visit."

"Look at this one, Hannah!" Gina picked up a deep medium yellow and held it up beside her face, near one of the curls bobbing over her temple. The color brought out the rich red-gold highlights in her brown hair and made her brown eyes gleam with gold specks.

"That one suits you very well," Hannah said, hesitating before she stepped closer. She was aware that the shopkeeper wasn't sure about her, and Hannah sensed that if she'd entered the shop without Gina, Mrs. Shaw may have turned around and disappeared into her back room, effectively refusing to serve her.

The rumors about her must have reached every ear in the village, Hannah thought ruefully. They all believed she'd been ravished by some man and then abandoned on the road where the dowager found her.

Her previous good spirits evaporated. Once again, she felt shaky and ill with weariness. Her hands felt cold and damp, despite her gloves, and she rubbed them over her arms. She shouldn't have agreed to come. It was foolish. In fact, she'd be fortunate if she didn't become ill again as a result.

"Do you have any blue ones that might match Miss Cowles's eyes?" Gina asked. Her busy fingers had set aside a green ribbon as well as the yellow one and were now sifting through the other colored strands.

"There's a few blue," Mrs. Shaw replied grudgingly. She pulled out a silvery blue and a medium blue ribbon from the increasingly tangled pile.

Gina picked up the medium blue one and held it up to Hannah's face. "This one would look so much better than those fusty old black ribbons, if you insist on wearing that bonnet. You should purchase it!"

Hannah flushed and caught Mrs. Shaw's knowing glance. She didn't have any money of her own at the moment. Or even a gown. Every garment she wore was a cast-off from the dowager.

"I know!" Gina clapped her hands and then pulled at the strings of her reticule. "It shall be my present to you! A welcome gift!" She looked at Hannah, her eyes warm with sympathy. "You cannot refuse, you know. It simply isn't done!"

Gina proceeded to haggle over the three ribbons, driving the price down so low that even Hannah was surprised that Mrs. Shaw agreed. Apparently, there were very few souls who could resist Gina's high spirits. Or her determination.

Shopping successfully concluded, Gina linked arms again with Hannah, gave her an assessing look, and yanked her once more down the street. "I believe we should see if my uncle Carter is at home. I am *famished* and absolutely faint with exhaustion, although you appear ready to walk to China if need be."

"Not quite China," Hannah protested with a laugh. "And you really shouldn't have bought that ribbon for me."

"Nonsense. It was a welcome gift. You have set foot on England's rocky shore for the first time—and under not so very pleasant circumstances, I might add—so it is time *something* agreeable happened to you."

"A great many very pleasant things have happened to me!" The image of Blackwold leaning over her last night, his linen shirt open at the neck, and his warm lips pressed against her forehead returned. Her cheeks grew warm. "Your grandmother—"

"Grandmother!" Gina snorted. "She only does what it amuses her to do. Not that we don't all adore her," she added hastily.

"You have all been exceptionally kind to me—more kind than I deserve," Hannah replied. Warm tears pricked her eyes, and she blinked rapidly. "I don't know what I would have done without your family and your grandmother in particular." She managed a laugh, although her throat was tight with emotion. "Why, I wouldn't have a stitch to wear if it were not for her."

"Pshaw." Gina made a rude noise. "She only gave you things which even Mary would not accept. Have you *looked* at the waistline of that walking dress you are wearing? Thank goodness the pelisse hides its worst faults. That dress must be fifteen years old at the very least. It might even be older than I!"

"It looked very nice to me, and Mary did a marvelous job remaking it. I have absolutely nothing to complain about."

"Then you colonists either have no sense of fashion, or you lag behind us by twenty years."

Straightening, Hannah sucked in a sharp breath. The Blackwold clan certainly could not be faulted for being too meek.

Gina laughed, squeezed Hannah's arm, and gave her a quick kiss on the cheek. She seemed to be forever kissing people as if to wipe away the unhappy effect of her words, but Hannah really couldn't stay mad at her.

"I'm sorry, but it is only the truth," Gina said, not sounding at all apologetic.

An unwilling smile curved Hannah's mouth. "You are forgiven. However, you might try to be a little more, um, *discreet* if you plan to attend many social events in London."

"You sound just like Grandmother." Gina giggled. "As if *she* had any room to criticize. She is even more horribly outspoken than I."

"Well, you don't want to be given the cold shoulder because you speak without consideration, so you might want to consider that."

"You don't think I might not earn a reputation for being *refreshingly honest*? I think it might be to my advantage, truly."

"With certain people, perhaps, though I'm not sure they are the sort you would wish to court. They would have to cherish no social ambition whatsoever."

"Or consider that marrying the cousin of a marquess is an exalted enough position to not care what anyone else thinks," Gina said in a surprisingly mature way.

Hannah frowned and glanced at her, wishing that the girl were not so aware of Society's realities. It would be nice if she maintained some illusions and ideals. It would be even nicer if she could fall in love like a normal girl without worrying about the opinion of Society.

Unfortunately, Gina was already aware that she was going to London to attract an alliance with someone of sufficient rank to earn her family's approval. Liking would be a benefit, but marriage would ultimately be more of a business affair than an affair of the heart.

So perhaps it was best that she didn't suffer from any illusions, after all.

Again, Hannah couldn't help a wistful thought of Blackwold. He, too, was in the midst of contract negotiations for the business of marriage.

So why did her thoughts turn to him, again and again?

She was nothing in his eyes—she couldn't even prove who she was in order to gain access to the money her father's lawyer had transferred here for her. Her chest tightened, leaving her breathless. It was so unfair—to lose everything, including her friends, her money, and her reputation in one terrible night.

For a moment, she wished she'd never decided to come to England to see the home of her father and find a place where she could belong. She should have stayed in Boston like the scruffy, elderly lawyer recommended. She could have made a home for herself there, even if she found the streets too busy and noisy for her taste.

"Here we are," Gina announced, releasing Hannah's arm. She opened the white-painted gate and stepped through onto a narrow path that led to a modest cottage.

Hannah glanced around, noting the small, stone church next door. So, this tidy little house with the winter-bleak front yard was the vicarage. The building looked well-maintained and neat, with a solemn, black-painted door and black shutters framing the windows, but it didn't feel welcoming to Hannah. Perhaps it was simply her sour mood and exhaustion after their long walk.

To her surprise, before they reached the two shallow, gray stone steps leading to the stoop, the front door opened.

Henry Hodges stood framed in the doorway, one hand setting his hat on his head.

"Cousin Henry!" Gina exclaimed. "Are you visiting Uncle Carter, too?"

He glanced at her, his brows arching in surprise before he saw Hannah standing a little ways behind her. "Ladies— I did not realize you were planning a trip to the village." Concern tightened his mouth and brow. "Miss Cowles, I am surprised to see you so soon after your illness." He sketched a brief bow. "Though, of course, you are looking as lovely as ever. You should have informed me of your intentions. I could have driven you here."

"We are not that helpless, Cousin," Gina said with a laugh. "It is only a mile."

A movement in the hallway beyond Mr. Hodges made Hannah glance inside the house. The first thing that caught her gaze was a large, rectangular object with curved sides. She stared, her heartbeat quickening.

My trunk! Her glance flew to Mr. Hodges's face.

A fleeting expression rippled over his features, one she couldn't quite identify.

"Where is Uncle Carter? There is no reason for us to stand out here gaping at one another. We are exceedingly tired and would like a cup of tea." Gina pushed past her cousin. "What is this trunk doing here? I almost fell over it—how inconsiderate of you to leave this nasty thing right in the middle of the hallway."

Mr. Hodges smiled, his gray eyes glimmering as he bowed again to Hannah and gestured for her to enter in front of him. "It is a surprise for Miss Cowles, my little goose. Though I wish you hadn't spoiled it."

"Uncle Carter!" Gina squealed and threw herself at a black-clad man standing just beyond the trunk. "Are you pleased to see us?"

He smiled and gave her a stiff-armed hug. "I am always pleased to see you, my dear. However, I know you have better manners than these. Who is this charming young lady?"

"That is Miss Cowles," Gina answered. "From Boston. In the United States of America."

"Yes, I know where Boston is located. Perhaps better than you, so behave yourself, Georgina." He bowed to Hannah. "And since my niece seems incapable of completing this introduction, may I present myself? Carter Hodges, Vicar of Pencroft, at your service, Miss Cowles."

The dim light of the hallway revealed a tall, slender man with dark hair cut very short and shot with silver at the temples. Another patch of silver sprouted from the hairline above the center of his forehead, and for an instant, Hannah was reminded of a skunk she'd glimpsed once. She stifled the ridiculous thought and smiled at him. He had gray eyes like his nephew, Henry, but a much more serious expression, and deep lines bracketed his mouth. A griffin ring on his right hand caught a flash of light from the small window next to the front door. This one had topaz eyes that glinted a dull yellow when he moved his hand.

His thin shoulders sloped down from his long neck, making him look like a man forced to carry a heavy burden, or perhaps the burdens of others, given his occupation.

"I am so sorry to intrude," Hannah said, feeling uncomfortable in the narrow confines of the little hallway.

Henry had entered behind her and closed the door, dimming the light in the cramped space. She pressed her hand to her chest. It was ridiculous, but it felt as if all the air was slowly being drained away, stifling her. Her toes practically touched the side of her trunk, Gina stood a mere yard away, with Carter Hodges just a foot beyond her. She glanced up to find Carter's eyes fixed upon her.

Not only was she being ridiculous, she was being rude. She forced a smile.

"I am always pleased to have a visit from my niece, especially when she brings such a lovely visitor with her," the vicar replied. His voice was so precise and measured that it had all the emotional resonance of a ticking clock.

She could only imagine how inspiring he would be giving a sermon in that voice and be relieved that no one had insisted she attend the small church.

"Is this indeed your trunk, Miss Cowles?" Henry asked as he swept off his hat. He placed it in the crook of his arm and gave her an encouraging smile.

For some reason, she felt embarrassed. Everyone was staring at her, mouths partially open and brows arched with enquiry. Self-conscious, she pulled her shawl up around her shoulders and leaned over to peer at the chest.

Saltwater had darkened the leather and left wandering trails of white salt behind. Some of the brass tacks securing the leather were missing, and parts of the leather covering were peeling. Despite the tarnishing of the brass, her initials were still clear, however.

She straightened. "Yes." She touched the brass plate with her gloved fingers. "These are my initials."

"How wonderful!" Gina clapped her hands before gripping her uncle's sleeve, though she glanced at her cousin. "How did you find it, Cousin Henry?"

"It was brought here for our sale," the vicar stated in his clockwork voice. "We are in need of roof repairs."

"Who brought it?" Hannah asked.

"Does it matter?" Henry replied in a hearty voice. "The important point is that your wish has been granted, and you have been reunited with your trunk."

"What's in it? Oh, I wager there are all sorts of beautiful gowns. Can we open it?" Gina asked, stooping over the box.

A curious reluctance filled Hannah, but she reached up to pull a chain out of her bodice. By some miracle, she hadn't lost the key—it had been forgotten at the bottom of her linen pocket—despite everything that had happened. And to avoid any mishaps, she now carried it with her wherever she went.

"I have the key," she admitted. Then she realized that the chain wasn't quite long enough to slip over the bonnet she wore.

Gina reached over to help her, but only succeeded in tangling the chain with the black ribbons holding the bonnet on Hannah's head. The result was that she almost strangled Hannah before the vicar pulled her away.

"Georgina! Please show your friend some courtesy. There is no reason to insist she open the trunk now," Carter chided her, his face growing stern.

"No—I need to open it. I need to prove that I am who I say I am." Hannah undid the ribbons of her bonnet and pulled it off. She then drew the chain over her head and knelt in front of the trunk.

The waves had not made what had always been a stiff lock any looser, but after some fumbling and twisting, she managed to undo the lock. Gina, shouldering her way past her cousin and uncle, knelt and unfastened the leather strap nearest to her.

"You had the key and unlocked the trunk, surely that is proof enough," Carter said.

"There is one more thing," Hannah said.

Her fingers were as cold and stiff as the lock and, although she rubbed them, her hands refused to cooperate. Finally, she took off her gloves, massaged her icy hands, and began the intricate process of opening the secret panel built into the domed lid. Small pieces of wood slid from one location to another in a mosaic before she felt the last slat move solidly into place.

A lid within the lid opened. There, resting in the narrow hollow was a small bundle of documents, securely wrapped in a thick piece of oilskin fabric and tied with sturdy string.

She lifted the packet out and held it up. "You see? These will prove who I am—and you saw me open the compartment—no one else knew the secret. And once we arrive in London, I can present my lawyer's letter to the manager at the Bank of England, and I can become quite independent." She flushed with pleasure at the thought. No more cast-off gowns, no more depending upon others for every little thing.

"Indeed." Carter nodded. "If required, we can, indeed, act as your witnesses, Miss Cowles. You had the key to the trunk and opened it. And you knew how to retrieve your package from the hidden compartment. I, for one, am thoroughly satisfied that you are who you say you are." He glanced at Henry. "If there had ever been any doubt."

"And I agree with my uncle, Miss Cowles," Henry said with a smile. The smug satisfied expression on his face gave Hannah pause, but she finally decided he was simply happy to have the problem of her identity resolved so easily.

"You mentioned the Bank of England, Miss Cowles," the vicar watched her steadily. "The manager is an associate of my brother—Georgina's father. We will send word to him that you have arrived safely so that you may obtain an accounting of the funds your trustees transferred for your use."

A tightening in her belly revealed a tinge of disquiet. Her lawyer in Boston had suggested that she wait for confirmation of the successful transfer of the majority of her fortune before she left, but she had just laughed. She refused to wait another month or more just to receive yet another letter.

She'd shaken off the twinge of uneasiness then, and she ruthlessly crushed the feeling again. She nodded. "That would be kind of you and Mr. Hodges, though we shall most likely reach London before any reply reaches us here."

"No doubt," Carter Hodges agreed in a patronizing tone that suggested he believed she didn't quite understand his caution, and that since she was only a female, he didn't actually expect her to.

"Who cares about some old papers? What's *inside?*" Gina wailed, her hands resting on the edge of the trunk's lid. "Do you have a great many dresses? Jewelry?"

"True heroine that she is, she managed to save her jewelry in the midst of the storm," Henry replied. His gray eyes twinkled with amusement. "And her dresses are no concern of yours, my little goose."

"You must have some tea after your long walk." The vicar shook his head. A long, lugubrious sigh escaped him. "A serious risk to your health so soon after your illness, Miss Cowles." He gave his niece a reproving glance. "It was not kind of you, Georgina, to force your friend to attend you, simply to see what ribbons Mrs. Shaw might have."

Georgina flushed and stared down at the floor, shifting from one foot to the other.

Stepping closer to her and slipping an arm around her waist, Hannah said, "Oh, I insisted. After being indoors for so long, the fresh air was a blessing."

"It is kind of you to say so," the vicar replied, his gaze still firmly fixed on his niece's downcast face. "Nonetheless, you must join me for tea before my nephew returns you to Blackrock Manor. We have the use of a trap when I require it, and there is no reason why Henry cannot drive you to Blackrock Manor in it." He eyed his nephew. "In fact, he may go to the inn now, while you have your tea."

Henry chuckled and gave Hannah a bow as he placed his hat on his head with a jaunty tap. "I shall return with your carriage—"

"Trap," the vicar corrected. "It will, however, accommodate the three of you, I assure you."

"Anon," Henry concluded, ignoring his uncle. "I am away, then, on winged feet."

With stooped shoulders and a heavy sense of doing one's duty, onerous though it may be, Hannah followed a very quiet Gina into the small sitting room on their left. The room was surprisingly austere—there were no comfortable padded chairs in sight, only five straight-backed wooden chairs. The chairs did have thin cushions on them, made out of some stiff dark material that, while practical, didn't look at all appealing. A small writing desk and another wooden chair were positioned by the window, and a low square table sat in front of the fireplace, between a pair of the wooden chairs.

The vicar pulled a third chair away from the wall and positioned it next to the chair on the left of the table. Then he gestured for Gina and Hannah to be seated.

"I will notify Mrs. Anderson that we have guests." He left them abruptly, just as they were sitting down.

"My uncle has a great deal on his mind," Gina said, fidgeting with the strings of her reticule. "The roof of the church is in a terrible state."

"I'm sure it is," Hannah replied, wondering when they could decently get up and leave.

It would probably be unforgivably rude to go outside to wait for Henry at the curb.

"Mrs. Anderson makes very good scones, though. She puts currants in them," Gina remarked, staring at her lap. "I hope you didn't think I was terrible when I wanted to see your gowns." She sniffed and gave Hannah a sideways glance. "I just can't seem to help myself when I am overcome with a fit of curiosity."

Hannah laughed. "Don't apologize—it didn't bother me in the least, and I know precisely what you mean. I would have been wrestling open the trunk, myself, had I been in your position. Curiosity may have killed the cat, but at least she died with a smile on her face."

"Thank you—you are such a dear friend. I just *knew* you would be!" Gina reached out and gave Hannah's wrist a squeeze.

A man's firm footstep interrupted them, and the vicar strode into the room. They half-rose from their seats and then sat down again as Carter flicked the tails of his black coat out of the way and seated himself in the chair opposite them. A long minute of silence reigned while he studied the two women. The clicking of the simple wooden clock on the mantle sounded so loudly that Hannah almost flinched.

The patter of lighter footsteps finally broke the uncomfortable quiet. Bearing a large tray, a woman entered, the ends of her apron sash fluttering behind her. She moved with brisk competence and unloaded the contents of the tray onto the maple table before straightening and smoothing her white apron.

"Is there anything else, Mr. Hodges?" she asked in a way that suggested that his answer had better be *no*. A white cap was set neatly on her graying black hair, and everything about her seemed to be in shades of gray, black, or white. Her dress was black, relieved by the white of her collar, cuffs, apron, and cap. Her dark hair was pulled back into a tight knot at the base of her neck, and the gray strands at her temples almost matched the hue of her eyes.

She appeared to be a stern, dour woman of the same stamp as Mary, until Hannah caught her gaze. Blue and silver flashes in her eyes hinted at a pleasant disposition, and she was surprised when the housekeeper gave her a quick wink.

"No, Mrs. Anderson," the vicar replied dutifully.

"The scones are fresh from the oven—they are best when warm," she said before turning on her heel and striding out of the room.

The vicar passed around the plate of scones, along with a pot of clotted cream, while Gina poured the tea into the plain white cups provided. To Hannah's surprise, Carter liberally applied the cream to his own scone before taking a large bite. Somehow, she thought he was the type of self-sacrificing, austere man who would refuse to allow himself to indulge in such luxuries.

"So, Miss Cowles, I was sorry to hear that your introduction to our shores was so tumultuous," he remarked after swallowing. He picked up his cup and took a sip, his eyes fixed on her face above the rim.

"Yes." Hannah picked up her cup and took a sip. The tea was warm and soothing, precisely what she needed. "It was not an experience I wish to remember."

He shook his head. "Of course. But was there no one to offer any assistance? The folk of our little village may be somewhat rustic, but they are well-known for their generosity as well as the kindliness of their spirit. Was there no one on shore to help you?"

"No." Hannah picked up her scone and took a large bite to avoid a lengthier discussion.

The questions reminded her of Blackwold and her unwilling admission. Why did everyone insist on knowing if she'd seen anyone? Did they imagine she would try to report the wreckers to the authorities?

If so, didn't that imply that they were in league with the wreckers?

A frown pinched the skin between her brows. If that were the case, why didn't they simply cut her throat and be done with it? The men she had seen on the beach didn't strike her as the sort who would be overly concerned about murdering an innocent woman, regardless of what she had, or had not, seen.

"Miss Cowles is going to go to London with me for my Season!" Gina blurted out, her teacup rattling in its dish as she placed it on the table in front of her. "Isn't it exciting?"

"Indeed," her uncle replied. He studied Hannah. "You saw no lights? No one coming to the shore to assist the survivors?"

"I saw nothing but wind and waves. The storm made it impossible to see anything else. And apparently, there were no other survivors."

"No. They brought the poor souls to my church. We interred them as best we could in the churchyard, though I'm afraid there is to be but one headstone for all of them."

A lump formed in Hannah's throat, and a sense of deep loss filled her. She swallowed several times and took a sip of tea to wash down the crumbs, almost choking on the scone, delicious though it was with the rich, thick clotted cream melting into the soft, steamy interior.

"It was such a tragedy," she said at last. "I cannot think about it."

"Of course not," he agreed, though his intent gaze belied his words. He clearly wanted very much to talk about the wreck of the *Orion*. "It is simply that one hears such tales after an event. And I am sure you do not appear to be the sort of young lady who would—well, enough said on the subject. My niece is clearly consumed by thoughts of her upcoming presentation and bow to Society. And I am sure you must be relieved to have your belongings restored to you, Miss Cowles."

"Yes, though I'm sorry you shall lose any profit you may have earned from the sale of them." She leaned forward. "I would be honored to make a donation for the repair of the church roof."

The vicar laughed stiffly, his lips barely moving. "It is not necessary, Miss Cowles. We will find the funds somehow."

"No, I insist. You have kept my trunk safe and returned it to me, and I would like to do this to thank you."

"Really, I would not expect such a sacrifice." Despite his words, his gray eyes gleamed. She could almost see him evaluating the possible size of her fortune.

Well, she felt no desire to enlighten him. She smiled demurely. "Nonetheless, I will send you something. A small token. To thank you for your gracious welcome and the return of my trunk." *Not to mention all the rumors you've been happy to spread about me wrestling with some man at the edge of the cliff.*

The vicar wisely let the subject go, and they talked about Gina's London Season until Henry returned, his face flushed from the cold air.

"Are you ready to return to Blackrock?" he asked from the doorway. A draft of chilly air blew in around him, ruffling the hems of their skirts.

Gina and Hannah leapt to their feet and gave Carter a hasty goodbye.

As they climbed into the trap, the two girls sitting with their backs to Henry, Hannah reflected that perhaps it was not such a sad thing that Carter Hodges neglected his grandmother. At least it was unlikely that there would be more such uncomfortable and tedious teas in the future.

Her recent illness also had one unexpected benefit; it was entirely likely that she could suffer from regrettable relapses of her illness, inexplicably occurring on Sundays.

Chapter Eleven

Out riding, Blackwold brought his horse to a halt and watched the trap heading toward Blackrock. Even at this distance, he could make out the slender figure of Hannah, topped by a ridiculous old black bonnet of his grandmother's. He grinned, and his hands tightened on the reins as a desire to join the group filled him.

His horse, sensing the quickening of his interest, moved in the direction of the road, and he had to bring the mare, Hera, to a stop. Hera snorted and danced sideways, wanting to continue forward to join the old chestnut horse pulling the trap.

"You're as bad as I am—wanting all the wrong things, eh girl?" He patted her neck and turned her around to gallop over the pasture sloping away from the cliffs behind them and the road bordering the other side.

The devil of it was, that despite everything else on his mind, his thoughts continued to stray to Hannah's smiling face.

He rode for another hour, tiring Hera, before easing her down the trail to the beach. Searching along the beach for more debris from the *Orion* and any clues left behind by the wreckers, he reviewed what little Hannah had told him. A broken mast and huge pieces of the hull had washed up, along with bits of rope, a few bottles, and even a waterlogged bible that was too far gone to salvage. He studied the wreckage before climbing back up on Hera and guiding her up one of the steep paths leading to the cliffs from the small, secluded beach.

His early morning interview with Hannah had confirmed his concern that she'd been a witness to the bloody activities that night. His brow wrinkled in deep thought as he rode back to the house. The distinct impression that she hadn't told him everything about the sinking of the *Orion* plagued him.

She didn't trust him, that much was obvious. And really, why should she? She didn't know any of them very well, and the Hodges were not known for being sensible or comfortably commonplace.

By the time he'd returned to the house and ensured that Hera was properly taken care of, the female members of the small party he'd seen on the road had disappeared indoors. Henry, however, had set out again almost immediately to drive the trap back to the inn.

Aware that the odor of horses and barnyards lingered around him, Blackwold ambled upstairs to wash and don a less fragrant set of clothes. His valet informed him that the dowager and the young ladies were in the Rose Drawing Room on the first floor, and Blackwold didn't bother to resist his desire to join them.

"Where have you been?" his grandmother greeted him in a querulous, shaky voice.

He glanced at her, his brows raised in mild surprise before his incipient grin turned into a frown. Her brown eyes appeared sunken into deep hollows, and her normally ruddy complexion had turned gray, emphasizing the deep wrinkles around her mouth and eyes.

If her voice hadn't alerted him, her appearance certainly did. She was not at all well, and, as usual when she didn't feel up to snuff, she showed signs of extreme irritability.

"I was out riding." He shoved his hands into his pockets and sauntered into the room. "I see the ladies have returned from Pencroft. How many ribbons did you buy from Mrs. Shaw this time, Georgie?"

Georgina rolled her eyes and let out a long sigh. "It's Gina, as you well know, Blackwold. How would you like it if I persisted in calling you something dreadful?"

"Like what?" he asked with evident interest.

"How should I know?" Georgina raised her hands in a helpless gesture of exasperation. "Blackie, or Woldy, or Moldy-woldy, perhaps."

"Those don't sound so very terrible to me." His mouth twisted into a lopsided grin. "You're free to use whichever pleases you—you have my permission."

"Well, thank you *ever* so much. I'm just *so* grateful."

Watching Georgina and Blackwold, Hannah held her hand in front of her mouth, trying not to laugh, but her blue eyes twinkled with merriment. Blackwold caught her gaze and winked.

A blush flooded her cheeks with color, and she hurriedly glanced down at her lap.

"Will you children stop being so nonsensical? You will call your cousin Georgina, Blackwold. And you, Georgina, will show your cousin the respect due his title."

"And I believe I will call for the doctor, Grandmother," Blackwold said. "It appears we are not free quite yet of all sickness at Blackrock."

"What do you mean by that?" the dowager demanded, straightening in her comfortable wing chair.

"There is no need to send for the doctor," Hannah added hurriedly. "I am quite well. All I needed was some fresh air, and our trip to the village provided that. Why, I am not even as tired as I expected to be, since we were able to stop at the vicarage for tea."

Blackwold smiled at her. "I am relieved that you are well, but it is not your health that concerns me." He turned his head to stare at his grandmother. "You, my dearest grandmother, are attempting once again to prove your resolve and iron constitution by not admitting when you are a trifle under the weather—"

"How *dare* you try to tell *me* what I do or do not feel?!"

"Well, that certainly explains it," Georgina said, as if she'd known all along that something was wrong. "You know you always get irritable when you are not feeling well, Grandmother." She caught the dowager's angry look and rushed to add, "Not that anyone could have noticed such an infinitesimal change in your mood. You are quite as pleasant as ever—isn't she, Hannah?"

Frowning, Hannah studied Lady Blackwold. "You do appear pale. I hope I haven't made you ill—I could never forgive myself if you became sick because of me."

"I am *not* ill and certainly not because of you, Miss Cowles," the dowager said, glaring at all of them. Two hectic splotches of anger colored her cheeks, but instead of giving her a healthy appearance, the redness only accentuated the dark circles under her eyes and the grayness of her skin. Even her lips had developed an unhealthy purplish-blue hue that hinted that she was not at all well.

"Then you won't mind a visit from Dr. Burland. Though, I must say, I don't think Miss Cowles actually tried to make you ill."

"What?" The dowager straightened. "Of course, she did not. Why would you say such a nonsensical thing?"

"I am not the one who suggested it." He held up a hand, forestalling the blistering comment that obviously waited upon his grandmother's fierce tongue. "No matter. I will send for Burland, and in the meantime, you should consider retiring to get some rest."

"I will not have that quack in this house!"

Blackwold's brows rose. "I thought you approved of Burland. Didn't you send for him to attend Miss Cowles?"

"That's different—she is young." Lady Blackwold's tremulous hands began rubbing back and forth along the padded arms of her chair as she stared into the fire blazing on the hearth. She refused to look up at him, even when he stepped closer. "I will not be bled, do you understand me? I will *not*!"

Blackwold placed a hand on her fragile shoulder and gave it a gentle squeeze. "I know you have a horror of blood; if we hide it from view—"

"No! I will not allow it."

"But Grandmother," Georgina said, interrupting. "Look how much good it did Hannah? If you are ill—"

"No!" The dowager's grip on the arms of her chair tightened, the thick blue veins standing out starkly under the paper-thin skin of her hands. "I will retire, and you may send for your Dr. Burland, if you wish, but he will not drain me of blood, the despicable leech."

"Very well. As long as you allow him to see you, I suppose that is sufficient," Blackwold acceded to her request. At least she agreed to see a physician and get some rest.

He'd often suspected that a good bowl of broth was just as efficacious as being bled, or perhaps more so, since it didn't leave one feeling wobbly-kneed and light-headed. However, he wasn't a medical man and would be the last one to assume he knew anything about curing disease.

The dowager's pallid complexion worried him, nonetheless, as he watched her stand, clutching Hannah's arm.

"You will not go to London without me, Blackwold. You shall just have to remain here a few more days until I am ready to travel," his grandmother stated firmly, staring at him.

"But Grandmother—my *Season!*" Georgina wailed, grasping the dowager's free arm.

"You cannot be presented without me, so there is no point in crying about it," the dowager replied sharply as she shook off Georgina's hands. "And it will only be for a few days. I shall not remain abed long—you will see. A week at most."

"A *week?*" Georgina's voice rose. "Oh, please, say I can go anyway—you can always come later when you are feeling well again." Her eyes brightened, and she took hold of her grandmother's arm again. "Hannah can be my companion, and I *promise* we shall behave with perfect propriety."

"How can you promise to act with propriety when I am not there, when you cannot do so when I am?" the dowager said crossly, shaking off Georgina's hands once more.

"Oh, *please!*" Georgina begged, her eyes filling with tears.

Blackwold shouldered his cousin aside and nodded to Hannah. "Will you see that my grandmother gets some rest, Miss Cowles? And a cup of broth, perhaps." He grinned. "There always seems to be hot broth bubbling away in a cauldron by the fire in the kitchen. Some of that witch's brew might bring a bit of color back to her cheeks."

"If it doesn't poison me first! And how dare you speak of me as if I were not in the room!"

Blackwold chuckled and used the opportunity to kiss his grandmother on the forehead. The skin felt papery thin and burning hot. "Go on. The broth will be waiting for you before you even get to your room. The doctor will arrive shortly. For once, dear Grandmother, you shall be the one doing as you're told."

"Well, I never!" She glared at him, but despite her frown, her eyes sparkled with mirth—or fever.

"That is precisely the trouble, my dear. You've never in your life done as you ought. Dare I hope for an exception, now?"

The dowager elbowed him in the stomach as she stepped past him, dragging poor Hannah along with her. "You may dare whatever you wish, Blackwold. You are a marquess, and I have never seen *you* do anything otherwise."

"Then I come by my hardheadedness quite naturally," he called after her, his voice rich with laughter.

She waved her hand over her head as the two ladies passed through the door, and he watched them until they disappeared down the hallway. His smile slowly faded into lines of worry that tightened around his mouth.

His grandmother wasn't in the first blush of youth like Hannah, and the American girl had been ill enough to cause them several moments of concern. In fact, while Mary slept on a trundle bed nearby, he'd spent several hours one night sitting next to her bed, wishing he could do something more than simply place damp rags on her forehead to calm her raging fever. Lady Blackwold would never survive such an ordeal, and he wasn't prepared to do without her. She'd been a fixture and firm friend in his life ever since he could remember.

Of course, he knew she wouldn't live forever, but he'd hoped she'd be around a few more years. He needed *someone* to nag him and snort with disgust when he made an innocent comment or two. Someone who almost understood him.

The frown tightening his brow dug a bit deeper. No doubt, Lady Alice would be thrilled to at least pick up the role of general termagant and nag, though he doubted there would be any of his grandmother's spirited good humor underlying it. His thoughts strayed to Hannah.

Now *she* wouldn't hesitate to nag him at the appropriate times, if she could keep from laughing long enough to do so.

His tension eased a fraction. He rotated his shoulders and cocked his head to listen to the sounds of footsteps clattering overhead. Gradually, the sounds diminished. A door creaked open and then closed.

"Oh, can't you convince her to let me go to London, anyway?" Georgina begged after Blackwold had rung for the butler and requested the broth for the dowager and that someone be sent for the doctor.

"No, my pet, I cannot." The marriage papers awaited him in London. Even this small delay seemed like a godsend.

"You mean you *will not*." Georgina's lower lip stuck out and her dark lashes sparkled with the frustrated tears she'd shed a few moments earlier.

"Are you afraid all the eligible bachelors will be snapped up in the course of the next few days?" He grinned and tapped her gently on the chin with his fist.

She scowled at him and stepped away. "No, of course not."

"Do you have an assignation, then? An appointment that can't be missed?"

"Stop it! Why must you tease me so? I just want to enjoy myself, for once."

"Dances? Balls?"

"The Royal Menagerie at the Tower of London," Georgina said, clasping her hands. Her eyes shone with excitement. "The Hudson Bay Company gave us a Grizzly

Bear named Martin—I'm sure even Miss Cowles would like to see that!" Her smile slipped a fraction and she glanced away. "Although I do hate to see an animal in a cage. They always look so piteous."

"Your heart is perhaps too tender for such sights. You might be better off looking for birds in Hyde Park."

A flush rushed over Georgina's cheeks, leaving her looking almost as fevered as their grandmother. She pressed her lips together and shook her head, clearly embarrassed that he knew her secret. "Oh, we shall be too busy, I'm sure, to worry about such things."

While she may not have spoken about it, and indeed, had done her best to hide it, no one who had been around her for long could miss her interest in the natural sciences. Everything from the smallest ant to the twinkling stars in the night sky seemed to fascinate her, and strangely enough, she seemed utterly fearless in her pursuit of all things natural. Even spiders that made other women shudder or scream in terror only made Georgina bend down and fumble for the small magnifying glass she kept in her reticule. And her father encouraged her, at least as far as astronomy went, considering that to be a fine subject for any curious mind, regardless of sex.

Oh, she tried to hide it by expressing a great deal of fascination in gowns and personal adornment, but it was all just for show. Given a choice between going to a dress shop and sprawling on the ground with a magnifying glass, there was no doubt in his mind which alternative would win.

He could only hope that whoever their grandmother elected as Georgina's prospective bridegroom would be either just as curious as his wife, or else too blind to notice or care about her peculiarities.

To his relief, Georgina's concern for the health of the dowager eventually overcame her frustrations at remaining at Blackrock a while longer. Without another word, she hurried away to see if she could be of assistance in the sick room.

Blackwold's estate manager located him before he could escape, and he was soon absorbed in business, including the necessity of shoring up one of the bridges on the road leading out of Pencroft, which the storm had battered and made unsafe.

The mail brought additional news, which a lesser man might call bad. Lady Alice and her mother were leaving their estate a few days early to make their way to London. The proposed journey would take them through Pencroft, and although Lady Alice was too much of a lady to invite herself to stay at Blackrock, she mentioned that they would break their journey at the village.

The only polite thing to be done was to extend an invitation to the ladies to stay at Blackrock, even though the dowager was ill, and it would be next to impossible to keep Georgina from insisting on traveling with Lady Alice and her mother to London.

There'd be no keeping her at Blackrock, now, he thought as he dipped his pen in a pewter inkwell and tapped off the excess ink. His reply was brief and to the point, inviting the ladies to break their journey at Blackrock. He almost added, "And the devil take you," but he managed to end the sentence with a very firm period, instead.

Well, if she were going to be his wife, he'd better get used to her. Maybe she would grow more likeable with familiarity. Some women, like Mary, appeared sour and stern until sickness or some other tragedy revealed the soft heart underneath. Lady Alice might be similar. The dowager's illness might bring out the kindness and warmth in Lady Alice.

Or quite the reverse. He sighed and shook the sand off the letter before sealing it.

His future was rushing toward him at an alarming rate, and he supposed, like dozens of titled men before him, that he'd fumble his way through it somehow.

After all, there were always the cliffs if one desperately wanted a way out.

Amy Corwin

Chapter Twelve

"What time is it?" Hannah asked sleepily, propping herself up on one elbow to peer blearily at the clock on the mantle. "Wait! Don't tell me." She hid a yawn behind her hand and punched the pillows to prop herself up in bed. "Three in the morning. If one can call the dead of night morning."

There was precious little moonlight tonight, and although she could vaguely see the outline of Blackwold sprawled in the chair next to her bed, she couldn't make out his expression.

Not that she had to, she thought, recalling his last visit at this very quiet and very cold time of night. She shivered and adjusted her quilt a little higher, seeking its soft warmth. Although her nightgown—her very own gown this time—had suitably long sleeves and a high neck, the linen was too thin to grant her much protection from the penetrating, damp chill of her room.

"Have you remembered anything else?" Blackwold asked in a revoltingly cheerful voice for three in the morning.

She grimaced and picked up the phosphorous box on the bedside table to light the candle. It was bad enough to be awakened from a comfortable sleep without being unable to even see the person who had committed the dastardly deed.

"Here, allow me. If you go on that way, you'll set the bed aflame." He grabbed the box out of her hands and efficiently set to work lighting the candle next to her bed.

A golden flame slowly flickered into life, but its feeble light was hardly better than the previous darkness. The glow sharply defined his nose, cheekbones, and chin, while leaving his most important feature—his brown eyes—hidden in shadowy hollows when they weren't completely obscured by the wayward lock of hair that persisted in falling over his brow.

"Burning to death might prove to be more restful in the long run," Hannah commented, stifling another yawn behind her hand. She stared at him, frowning. "Why would I have remembered anything more? I told you everything the last time you forced your way into my bedroom."

Her irritation increased when he chuckled. He pushed the thick lock of hair back from his forehead, only to have it immediately fall forward again when he shifted in his chair. "Your trip to the village, my dear Hannah. The fresh air, or sights therein, might have touched some chord."

"Well, the only thing our walk managed to accomplish was to make me extremely tired."

"Not too tired, I hope. After all, you did manage to have tea at the vicarage. And good old Cousin Henry drove you back."

"It was exhausting enough, I assure you. Particularly after being ill."

He stiffened in his chair, and tension seemed to suddenly pool in the air between them. "And now Grandmother is unwell."

"You can't blame me for that!" Hannah exclaimed, straightening. "I did not mean to make her—or anyone—sick."

"No one is blaming you, Hannah," he replied absently, his right hand brushing an unseen speck of dirt off his black evening breeches. His dark blue jacket was open, revealing a cerulean blue waistcoat with silver embroidery and buttons, and although that remained closed, his neckcloth once again hung untied around his neck and his white linen shirt was open.

Her irritation melted away as the warmth of amused tenderness welled up inside her.

She relaxed a fraction and leaned back against her pillows, a small smile curving her lips. "How is she doing?"

"Not well." His hand brushed over his thigh once more before he let his arm fall to his side, letting the shadows hide the restless movements of his fingers. "The doctor wanted to bleed her, but she refused. She is resting, though."

"You're worried about her."

The muscles in his jaw clenched briefly before he smiled. "Of course. She may be a ferocious old woman, but if she develops a high fever..."

She won't die—she can't. The words almost rushed out of Hannah's mouth, but she clamped her lips shut. While the thought might be kind, the truth was, she could no more guarantee that Lady Blackwold would survive than she could make the rain go away.

"Is there anything I can do? Is anyone with her?" Hannah lifted her covers as she slid her feet out of bed.

Blackwold grabbed the covers with one hand and her ankle with the other and forced her back into bed, smoothing the quilt over her. "Yes. Mary is with her. That woman delights in having a patient to nurse. Sometimes I wonder if she doesn't encourage illness just to give herself a new invalid to fuss over."

Hannah laughed and pushed at his shoulder, forcing him away from the bed. His muscles felt hard under her touch. "I'm sure she doesn't wish sickness on anyone."

"No, though she positively revels in it when it does occur," he replied sourly. He slumped back in his wooden chair, one arm propped up on her bedside table and the other dangling at his side. "So, what did you think of our vicar?" he asked, changing the subject abruptly.

He reminds me of a skunk. She hid another burst of laughter behind her hand and forced a more serious, or at least calm, expression on her face. "He seemed very... meticulous."

He snorted and flung his head back to clear the lock of hair out of his eyes. "A great comfort to our villagers in time of need," he commented in a dry voice. "Just the sort you'd want to find next to your bed as you lay dying."

"Yes. Well..." She glanced away awkwardly, her hands picking at the edge of the quilt.

"Miserly old dog," he added in a soft voice. "Though I understand he recently hired a curate. Makes you wonder how he could afford the man. No doubt but that he'll work him to death, saving all the poor souls of the parish, while rewarding him with a generous income of slightly less than fifty pounds per annum. Or less, if he can manage it. A fine religious man, our uncle Carter. His love of God is only surpassed by his venality."

There seemed little she could say to contradict his cynical observation, particularly since she secretly believed it to be true. Though to be fair, she had no idea if the vicar was a miser or not. After all, he had given her back her trunk and even seemed reluctant to accept a monetary gift from her, although he apparently needed the funds for the repair of the church.

Perhaps there was some family incident in the past that had soured the relations between the two men. Whatever it was, Hannah had no right to interfere.

"He seemed kind," she murmured. She glanced up, smiling. "Did you hear that my trunk was found? Now there can be no question as to my identity."

"Indeed." His brown eyes glinted in the candlelight, but the shadows hid the nuances of his expression, making him appear only mildly interested. "And who made this momentous discovery?"

"Your cousin, I believe. Mr. Henry Hodges."

"Are you sure?"

"Of course." But a frown creased her brows as she reconsidered his question. The trunk had been at the vicar's house, and she couldn't precisely remember if anyone had actually claimed the responsibility for the discovery. "Or rather, I believe someone from the village may have actually found it and brought it to the vicar's home. They are apparently preparing for an auction, or something similar, to obtain the funds to repair the church roof."

"So, the trunk was at the vicarage?"

"Well, yes. They planned to auction off the contents." She flushed and glanced away, feeling awkward and slightly embarrassed, though she had no reason for such sensations. "I offered a small token. Of thanks." Her cheeks felt as if they were on fire.

"And did Uncle Carter accept your small token?"

"No—not precisely. That is, I must present my letter of introduction and so on to the Bank of England, where my lawyer arranged to transfer a sum for my use. I'm sure it can all be arranged once we go to London."

"I'm sure it can," he replied dryly.

"What do you mean by that?" She straightened, her hands gripping the edges of the quilt.

He slumped back further in his chair, his legs stretching out so far that they went under the edge of her bed. "Nothing. I'm sure my uncle will be suitably grateful for whatever token amount you wish to grant him."

Did he think she was a miser, as well? Or did he still believe she was an adventuress, out to cheat his grandmother? "That's a despicable thing to say! Get out! I'm exhausted and extremely tired of this conversation, as well."

He studied her, a half-smile twisting his mouth. "You don't enjoy our little *tête-à-têtes*?"

"How could anyone enjoy being awakened in the middle of the night to be interrogated and insulted?"

"I've insulted you?" His brows rose, disappearing under his shaggy hair. "I do apologize."

"You do not— I've never seen anyone less apologetic in my life."

His grin widened. "If you consider it, you'll realize it wasn't you I was insulting."

"No—it was your uncle—and me by implication. Why don't you like your uncle?"

"He's on the wrong side of the family."

"Wrong side?"

"Surely, our Georgina has explained." He chuckled. "I'm on the mad side, while dear Cousin Henry and Uncle Carter are... not."

Hannah laughed again. Her smile degenerated into another yawn, however, and she hastily hid that behind her hand. "How trying for you. I suppose your cousin and uncle must be great friends, then."

"Not particularly. Like repels like, or so I've been told."

"But Henry was at the vicarage."

"Yes, he was, wasn't he?"

Hannah studied his face. Once again, he seemed almost expressionless in the flickering light. "What was he doing there?" she asked.

"I was hoping you could tell me."

"I thought it was something to do with my trunk, but truly, I don't honestly know."

He sighed and placed a hand flat on the bedside table to push himself up. "No. More's the pity."

For a moment, he stood there at the side of her bed, towering over her. She held her breath, looking up at him, wanting him to lean over, wanting to feel the warmth of his chest and strength of his arms around her. Pools of darkness hid his eyes, but he seemed to be staring at her.

Slowly, he bent, one hand clasping the bedpost. A shiver of excitement went through her. Her eyelids fluttered, and her toes curled as she lifted her chin. There was one hushed moment when he paused, his mouth mere inches from hers. The heady fragrance of his skin, combined with a spicy bay and soap scent, made her take a deep breath.

His lips brushed hers gently before he moved to press another kiss against her forehead. "Sleep well, Hannah. And if you do remember anything, I hope you will share it with me."

"At three in the morning?"

His low chuckle whispered over his shoulder as he moved toward the door. "It *is* the best time for honesty, after all."

"Only if you're an owl." She watched as he slipped through the door.

A soft click, a few footsteps, and the quiet returned to the house, though not to Hannah. She couldn't forget the scent of him or the warm softness of his lips. Her body tingled with excitement, and when she tried to close her eyes and fall asleep, she couldn't.

Her thoughts kept whirling back to Blackwold and how *right* it had felt when he'd pressed that light kiss on her mouth.

It wasn't until dawn that her eyes snapped open with the thought that she'd met all the men who wore the griffin ring except one: Georgina's father.

One of them was the man who had ordered the death of Officer Trent, and for some reason, she wanted it to be the one person she hadn't yet met. She rolled over in bed and turned her pillow to the cool side. It would be awful if it turned out to be Georgina's father. Too awful to contemplate.

However, something even worse kept hovering around her like a suffocating fog. She wasn't sure, but she felt like she was on the verge—in fact, her toes were already sticking out over that line—of falling in love with a man who might be that murderer. And to make that horror even more tragic, he might even be engaged to someone else.

Chapter Thirteen

"She has told you nothing?" Officer Farley asked again, his hands clasped behind his rigid back and his nearly invisible brows rising toward the brim of his hat.

"She apparently saw very little, being occupied by the difficulties presented by the waves and wind," Blackwold repeated, staring past the Customs Officer's shoulder to the winding road leading back to Blackrock Manor. He contemplated pointing out that they wouldn't have needed to question Hannah if Farley hadn't sent him on a wild goose chase the very night that the wreckers had lured the *Orion* to her doom, virtually on Blackrock Manor's doorstep.

But there was no point in arguing about the past.

Farley frowned. "You said she saw the leader."

"His back. Backs are notoriously difficult to identify."

The officer had the grace to look abashed. He glanced down at the rutted dirt road and shifted his booted feet. "There is nothing else, my lord?"

"No. I have repeatedly questioned Miss Cowles. Her story has remained consistent. As I may have mentioned, if there is any additional information, I will send word to you. There is no need to meet otherwise."

"Yes, my lord." Farley pressed his hat more firmly on his head. "Much obliged, my lord." A cascade of polite thanks, mingled with obsequious apologies, erupted as Blackwold turned and walked away.

"Idiot," Blackwold muttered under his breath as he rounded the curve in the road before the drive straightened to lead directly to Blackrock's massive stone portico, sheltering the front door.

The sight of the manor, ungainly though it might be with various additions jutting out at odd angles, chimneys dotting the jumble of roofs, and the seemingly random placement of windows, never failed to make him smile. It seemed as rumpled and comfortable as an old jacket.

Home.

Instead of going in the front door, he walked around to the stables. A ride would clear his head and perhaps allow him to develop another strategy for identifying the man responsible for so many tragic deaths. While he enjoyed his three a.m. talks with Hannah, they were proving to be less helpful than he had hoped.

Nonetheless, he had the niggling thought that she'd seen more than she was willing to admit. If only she trusted him...

The frantic activities of two grooms, running thither and yon in the stable yard caught his attention. Increasing his pace, he strode through the gate and caught the youngest man, Jim, by the arm.

The groom turned a pale face to him. Sweat beaded his brow as he gulped for air. He blinked, recognized Blackwold, and grew so white that the freckles on his face stood out starkly.

"My lord!" he yelped.

"What has happened?"

"It be that mare—Hera."

"Hera?" A knot clenched his gut. While generally docile, the horse was easily spooked. "Was anyone injured?" He grabbed the young man's flapping waistcoat. "One of the women?"

Jim's eyes rolled up in his head, flashing white in the sunlight.

For a moment, Blackwold thought he was going to faint, and he gave the groom a shake before repeating, "Is anyone injured?"

"Don't know, my lord," he moaned. "Gone—she be gone—clean as the wind."

"Gone?" He glanced around. The gate leading to the garden path hung open. He pushed the lad away. "Get a rope and bridle. *Now!*"

"Yes, my lord." The groom stumbled away.

Blackwold strode to the garden gate and waited. New green growth had appeared—vegetation a horse might want to investigate. Less than a minute later, Jim came running back, a rope and bridle hanging from his hands.

"Come with me," Blackwold said, grabbing the items from the groom and striding through the gate.

Halfway down through the garden he paused. The horse wasn't far away—he could hear the heavy thudding of hooves.

"The cliffs, my lord!" the groom exclaimed, pointing. "She be heading for the cliffs!"

Blackwold nodded and raced in that direction. The horse had too much sense to gallop over the edge, but he'd noticed that Hannah liked to walk along the path that followed the edge. She showed absolutely no fear of heights, which normally would be cause for admiration, but at the moment, only tightened the fist of anxiety strangling his gut.

Sure enough, when they cleared the last of the hedges bordering the garden proper, he saw the gray horse, Hera, neighing and cantering over the rough turf. Miss Cowles stood on the cliff path facing them and the horse.

Stay still! He prayed the horse hadn't seen her, hadn't noticed the white gown draping her solitary figure.

A gust of wind whispered around them, lifting the hair off his forehead. The hem of her gown rippled.

The horse, seeing the movement, jerked back a step. Snorting and rolling her eyes, Hera stamped the ground and then reared on her hind legs.

When he'd purchased the horse, she was described as very docile and well-behaved. And she was—as long as she encountered only men. There was something about women—and the flapping of women's skirts—that drove the animal mad with fear. He'd warned his family, and the ladies gave the horse a wide berth, but Hannah didn't know.

"Hera!" Blackwold called in a strong, calm voice, striding toward the animal. "Don't move, Miss Cowles. And keep your skirts under control."

He was too far away to see the expression on her face, but Hannah, apparently sensing danger, pulled and twisted her skirts into a tight corkscrew around her limbs.

Jim edged around Blackwold and began a flanking movement.

Dancing nervously, Hera pawed the earth and flung her head up. Once again, she eyed Hannah, for all the world as if trying to judge how best to force her over the cliff. The horse cantered a few more steps toward the woman and jerked violently again in response to another, stronger gust of wind.

The ribbons on Hannah's bonnet fluttered, and the hem of her shawl flapped.

Blackwold was almost to the horse. He could feel the heat pouring off the animal's flanks. Under her sweaty coat, her muscles rippled as she prepared to leap forward.

"I've got her by the mane, my lord!" Jim's voice called.

Hera reared again, flinging off the groom. Her front legs pawed the air before she dropped with a thud.

At that instant, Blackwold flung the rope around her neck and flung his arm over her neck. His arm swept around her head to hide her eyes. If she couldn't see Hannah, she wouldn't be afraid.

"Hera—easy, girl," he murmured into the horse's twitching ear.

The groom grabbed the bridle out of his hand and quickly shoved the bit into the horse's mouth. Blackwold moved the horse's head so that he could stand between the horse and Hannah, blocking the animal's view, all the while stroking her neck and murmuring soothing words.

"Get her back to the stable," he said when Jim finished adjusting the bridle.

"Yes, my lord." Jim turned to lead the horse back, careful to keep her facing away from the cliff.

"Wait—Jim. How did Hera get out of her stall?"

The groom looked at him, his dark eyes as white-rimmed and panicked looking as Hera's had been. "Sorry, my lord. I never seen—Tom and I just seen the door open—right before you came."

"Who else was in the stable? Or stable yard?"

"I—I doesn't know, my lord. Honest. Mr. Henry and the vicar arrived, and we was busy with their gig—we never saw what happened."

Once again, he was left wondering which of his male relatives might wish to arrange an accident for Hannah to prevent her from remembering anything useful. They all knew about Hera and her fear of women. Releasing the horse was sure to result in a tragic accident. There was always a stiff breeze sweeping in from the ocean, and they all knew Hannah's custom of walking along the cliff path. Her skirts were certain to flutter in the wind, and Hera could be depended upon to fly into a fit of terror at the sight, either killing Hannah outright with her hooves or sending her over the edge.

"Very good, Jim. Walk her around the yard before you rub her down. And lock the bloody stall door."

"Yes, my lord." Jim led the horse away.

Head hanging docilely, Hera followed Jim, the entire incident forgotten by the animal.

Blackwold turned to find Hannah hurrying toward him.

"What happened?" she asked. Her pale skirts fluttered in the brisk wind.

"Hera—that horse—got out of her stall. Like many of us, she has a horror of women." His mouth twisted wryly as he held out his arm and waited for Hannah to slip her gloved hand through.

"Horror, indeed." In an attempt not to laugh, she snorted, and her blue eyes twinkled as brightly as the clear sky beyond her. "It is a wonder to me that the British race can manage to survive at all if half the population maintains a horror of the other half."

"It is a miracle, is it not?" he asked with a bland expression fixed on his face.

"Miracle, indeed." She snorted and shook her head as he drew her toward the house.

He smiled and pressed her fingers against his arm. "Thank you for listening." Relief swelled in him when he considered what might have happened to the lovely woman walking next to him.

"You can thank my father—he taught us well when we were in the wilderness of North America. You learn very quickly when to obey and when to argue, or you are likely to find yourself in the embrace of a Grizzly Bear. Or worse."

"Is there worse?"

She shivered, and the corners of her mouth drooped. "Oh, yes. Rattlesnakes. I cannot abide poisonous snakes." Her voice grew low and somber. "My youngest sister, Eleanor, was struck by one. She perished—it was terrible."

"I'm sorry."

"It was a long time ago." Her words quavered with grief, and her grip on his arm tightened. Taking a deep breath, she glanced at him. "Why do you keep that horse if she is so dangerous?"

"I have no wish to see her put down. I believe, in time, I might be able to convince her to forget her fear." He shrugged.

"You are very kind. I wish you luck—I truly do."

They climbed the steps to the terrace in silence, and they were within a yard of the French doors when Georgina burst outside.

"Hannah! I have been waiting for you for ages! Grandmother has received the latest copy of *La Belle Assemblée*!" She grabbed Miss Cowles's hand and dragged her away from Blackwold. "Come—you must see—there is the most elegant mourning dress you can imagine!"

Bereft of Hannah's warmly generous company, Blackwold strolled into the library, only to be met by his secretary.

"The accounts, my lord," Harris reminded him, tapping the black leather cover of the ledger book he held. "If you would grant me a few moments of your time?"

"But Grandmother just received a new copy of *La Belle Assemblée*," he said, unable to resist.

Harris stared at him and then heaved a long-suffering sigh. "Yes, my lord. The accounts?"

"If you insist." This time Blackwold sighed before he followed his secretary obediently, wondering if pouring over fashion plates might not be preferable, all things considered.

Chapter Fourteen

Despite the dowager's illness, the next few days were halcyon ones spent under blue skies decorated with fluffy white clouds and temperate weather for March. Even the biting northeastern winds had eased into soft breezes. The path along the cliff called to Hannah, and she frequently walked there, despite the incident with Hera. The wide sky fascinated her and filled her heart with such a rush of longing that her breath caught in her throat. The moody weather shifted without warning from translucent blue to dark, gunmetal gray as brief storms raced in, rained, and then evaporated in the blink of an eye. Under the influence of the soft mist, the gently undulating countryside was rapidly turning to lush green, dotted with swaths of spring flowers that lent their soft fragrance to the near-constant breeze.

Hannah, Gina, and Blackwold spent most mornings riding over the lovely countryside—showing Hannah an England she'd truly come to love. Poor Hera was left behind, however, locked in her stall, with her head hanging over the door as if she, too, longed to go cantering over the rolling turf.

On Friday morning, they even managed to ride a few miles further afield, to the small village of Boscastle. The quay was a hive of activity, and many of the inhabitants seemed too engaged in the business of fishing to notice the trio of riders.

With a twinkle in his brown eyes, Blackwold recommended they visit the church. Hannah gazed at him, suspecting some sort of jest, but unable to see what it could possibly be. It was a church, after all. What could be amusing about that?

But in the cool, dimly-lit church, Blackwold solemnly pointed to the epitaph for the Rev. W. Cotton and his wife:

Forty-nine years they lived man and wife,

And what's more rare, thus many without strife,

The first departing, he a few weeks tried

To live without her, could not, and so died.

"Doesn't seem possible, does it?" Blackwold asked as they strolled out into the bright sunshine.

"I don't see why not," Hannah replied. "My own parents were very happy."

"For forty years?" Gina stared at her, waiting for her cousin to help her into the saddle. "Without any arguments?"

"Well, no, not forty years." Hannah arranged her skirts to fall gracefully over the sidesaddle and patted the warm neck of the dappled gray mare. "And they naturally had a few contretemps—all those who are married do so. However, I'm sure they would still be firmly attached to one another had they lived. Their quarrels rarely lasted long."

Her mare snorted and shook her head, restive and wanting to be on the way back. Hannah had noticed that the further they roamed from Blackrock Manor and the comfortable stables, the more restive the horse grew.

With Blackwold's assistance, Gina climbed onto her sidesaddle. She frowned as she fiddled with the reins. "But they married for love, did they not?"

"Yes," Hannah replied with a smile. "And they were very well suited. They were both fascinated with travel and could rarely be persuaded to stay in one place for very long."

Blackwold mounted his own horse, a magnificent bay with beautiful lines. "Then they were fortunate, indeed, to find each other. Love is generally the most ephemeral and fleeting of emotions, and one that rarely grows for long, even between those who are well suited." He gathered the reins and turned his horse's head toward Blackrock.

"Fleeting if one's emotions are shallow." Hannah stared at his straight back as she guided her horse to trot next to Gina's.

Did he truly believe what he said? The thought lowered her spirits, and her shoulders sagged. Even her mare seemed to plod along, head down in an exceedingly dispirited manner.

The last few nights, Blackwold had made such a habit of visiting her at the stroke of three that she found herself waking up in anticipation. Sadly, he'd also fallen into the habit of kissing her goodnight on the forehead, no matter how she lifted her chin and closed her eyes in the hopes that he felt the same attraction fluttering in his stomach that she felt in hers.

Perhaps he wasn't attracted to her at all and simply hoped she'd finally admit she'd seen the face of the man on the beach.

Then what would he do? Smother her with one of her pillows? The murderer was obviously either he or one of his relatives, so she could only anticipate the worst.

Well, what else had she expected? That he would fall in love with her and ask her to marry him?

For people like Gina and Blackwold, duty was held in the highest regard, and they would do as expected. They would set aside their emotions and marry to advantage and live well-ordered, dutiful lives. The thought made Hannah want to scream.

A quick glance at Gina's frowning face made her suspect that the girl wasn't enchanted by the prospect of doing her duty, either.

Duty... If that was so important to Blackwold, why had he brought them to Boscastle? Why show them that epitaph, that testament to the enduring power of love? Even if it were stated humorously, the epitaph nonetheless told the tale of a couple so devoted that one could not live without the other.

Her own parents had been the same. And how many others had also found life unsupportable when their helpmate perished?

That Blackwold would show her that epitaph and then continue to pursue his obligation to marry for duty rather

137

than love seemed to point to only one thing: that he had seen the affection she harbored for him in her eyes, but he didn't feel the same. That he didn't believe in the power of love.

This foray might have been undertaken, not for the sake of curiosity, but as a warning to her not to give him too dear a place in her heart.

By the time they trotted into the courtyard at Blackrock Manor, she was sick of her thoughts. Her frown matched Gina's as a groom helped them dismount, and her mood soured further when Henry wandered around the corner of the house.

"Miss Cowles!" he called, waving to them.

"Cousin Henry," Blackwold greeted him with a nod.

Henry replied, "Blackwold." Skirting Blackwold, he approached Hannah and offered her his elbow. "Grandmother has been asking for you." He glanced at the gray mare as the groom led her toward the stable. "If I had known you were going riding, I would have escorted you."

"No need," Blackwold said, interrupting him.

Shrugging, Henry maneuvered Hannah toward to the door. "Blackwold is so occupied these days, he barely has time for any of us. Poor Grandmother has been quite wretched and in need of distraction."

"But we have all been visiting her—I read to her yesterday afternoon for several hours," Hannah protested, her cheeks flushing. Someone was always attending to the dowager, hoping to amuse her and make her feel less miserable.

But she supposed that since Lady Blackwold was confined to bed, the hours went much more slowly and seemed a great deal more empty than they did for the rest of them.

Henry patted her hand where it lay within the crook of his elbow. "I am sure you've done a great deal. Her spirits were so low this morning that she felt particularly lonely and in need of your company. Though you've only been with us for a short time, I know she feels very attached to you. As we all do."

Flush deepening, Hannah tried to pull her hand away from his arm using the pretext of lagging behind him a step. His arm tightened, and he moved her forward insistently.

"I should change—I smell of the stables," she protested as they came to the wide staircase. "I will visit the dowager as soon as I refresh myself."

"Very well. I will let her know you have returned and will attend her shortly. You're very kind, Miss Cowles. We are so fortunate to have you here." Henry released his grip on her as they reached the second floor.

First floor, she amended silently. She had to remember she was in England now, and they designated the floors quite differently. "Thank you," she replied with a sigh. "I won't be long."

After making a quick toilet and pulling on a simple day dress in pale rose with matching pink shoes, she picked up the gothic novel she'd been reading to the dowager. Walpole's *The Castle of Otranto* wasn't precisely Hannah's preferred material—in truth it was a little long-winded— but Lady Blackwold seemed to enjoy Isabella's attempts to elude marriage to Manfred.

As she approached the dowager's door, it opened, and Henry stepped out into the hallway. He smiled when he caught sight of her. "Miss Cowles! Thank you again—my grandmother is eager to see you." With a shallow bow, he opened the door and held it for her. "Miss Cowles, Grandmother..."

"I can see her as well as you can, Henry," the dowager said. Her heavily veined hands straightened the thick blue quilt over her lap. Her ruffled white nightcap was tied securely under her sagging chin, and her bed jacket was a frothing sea of lace and elaborate white silk embroidery, giving her the appearance of a very elderly, wrinkled mermaid peering out from the foamy crest of a wave. "Close the door after you!"

"Yes, Grandmother." He bowed to both ladies, smiling at Hannah before disappearing into the hallway. The door closed with a soft snick of the lock.

"So, Miss Cowles, you've finally managed to pause in your pursuit of my grandson long enough to visit your poor, lonely benefactor."

Hannah stared at her, clutching the leather-bound book to her chest. Protesting that she was not pursuing Blackwold seemed absurd, and she refused to do so. "Your granddaughter and I just returned from Boscastle. We've been getting some fresh air. If you feel strong enough, perhaps you might like to go outside to get some air this afternoon. I'd be happy to assist you."

"Fresh air? Where are your wits, girl?" She leaned forward, her eyes fixed upon Hannah. "I am ill—do you wish to push me into my grave? Fresh air, indeed!"

Hannah gripped the wooden chair next to the small, elegant desk positioned in front of a window and pulled it closer to the head of the bed. "Would you like to continue *The Castle of Otranto*?"

"Yes—in a minute." The dowager's gaze dropped to her covers for a moment. She smoothed the quilt again, her hands moving restlessly. "I am not very strong, Miss Cowles. The doctor has been—he quite despairs of me."

"Nonsense. You are well on the road to recovery."

The dowager's eyes flashed. Her thin mouth tightened. "You are optimistic—that has always been one of the most egregious faults possessed by you colonists. One need only look at your ridiculous revolt to see the consequences of such an attitude. You never recognize a looming tragedy until it is upon you."

"It does seem to have worked out, however. And we are no longer colonists, Lady Blackwold. So, I don't believe optimism is a fault in need of correction. Quite the reverse."

"And I doubt you see the nose in the middle of your own face!" the dowager retorted, her face flushing an unhealthy magenta.

"Quite true." Hannah clasped her hands on top of the book resting in her lap. "Unless I happen to glance into a mirror, of course. Now, as I recall, Manfred had locked poor Theodore in a tower in the last chapter. Should I begin reading there?"

Lady Blackwold glared at her. "I haven't the slightest interest in whatever fate befalls that pathetic ninny!"

"Thank goodness," Hannah said, letting out a long breath. "*The Castle of Otranto* may have been very popular a few years ago, but I have to admit that I find it tedious. Is there another book you'd prefer?"

"No, there is not! I have no interest in spending the last few hours of my life listening to you read."

Hannah laughed. "You are not dying, I assure you."

"Everyone dies, young lady, as you will soon discover." The dowager cut off Hannah's protest with a wave of her hand. "And I have something I wish to discuss with you."

"Very well. I will do my best to respond intelligently."

"No intelligence is required, Miss Cowles. Just a good and honorable heart."

Hannah smiled and nodded, although a nervous flutter in her stomach made her clasped hands tighten.

"I have spoken to my grandson, Henry, several times about this situation. He has informed me that you have proven your identity to everyone's satisfaction." The dowager fixed her gaze on Hannah's face, as if to pin her to her chair. "And he agrees that since your father's title remains dormant, it may be possible for your husband to apply for and receive the title, based upon the original letters patent. This will have to be examined, of course, but I believe your husband will be able to lay claim to the original estates and so on if this proves successful."

"Perhaps, but I am not interested—"

"You may profess to a lack of interest, but the truth is, why else come to England? You are a young, moderately attractive woman—what other purpose could you have but to lay claim to what should have been your family's inheritance?" Her gaze fluttered to the blue quilt before focusing even more firmly on Hannah. "My Henry—he has received so little, has so few expectations and is far more deserving... Well, this is what I wished to discuss with you—my last request."

"But you are not dying, Lady Blackwold," Hannah pointed out with a smile.

"I am far more gravely ill than any of you suspect!" The dowager's eyes flashed, and her sagging chin quivered with emotion. "And I have only one request—one small thing to hope for."

Hannah's heart sank. She didn't want to hear the dowager's request. "Lady Blackwold—"

"Be quiet! We have opened our home, and I daresay our hearts, to you, and my dear Henry is not unattractive. He is a kind and generous man—*he* should have been Lord Blackwold if the fates had any sense whatsoever. And Blackwold can be such a fool, though we all adore him. In any event, I *will* have Henry comfortably settled. All I ask of you is your promise that you will agree to marry my Henry." She held up one shaking hand, demanding silence. "*He* is the one taking the risk, for there is no certainty that what should have been your father's title will be granted, along with any estates associated with it. However, he has insisted that he is prepared to shoulder the risk and responsibility. He holds you in great affection, Miss Cowles, and would make an excellent husband. Will you promise me—on this bible," she gestured to the black leather-covered volume on her bedside table, "that you will marry my Henry?"

No! Absolutely not!

Her thoughts screeched and whirled with revulsion at the idea. She could never marry a man she didn't love, and there was something about Henry Hodges that she couldn't trust. His vanity and self-satisfaction made him difficult to like, much less consider as a spouse.

"I am truly sorry, Lady Blackwold, but I can't."

The dowager stared at her, so angry that she literally shook. Her hands clutched and released the blue quilt over and over again.

Hannah leaned over and placed a hand on the dowager's arm, fearing an apoplectic attack.

Lady Blackwold took a deep, quivering breath and said through thinned lips, "It is all I ask of you, Miss Cowles. In return for the hospitality we have shown you. Is this how you show your gratitude? By refusing what may be your best—your only—hope of a secure future? I have heard the rumors from the village. Do you think you will find a better mate than my Henry? Are you that silly and blind? We are offering you security and the chance to establish yourself in your family's hereditary seat. Would you throw that all away because of your stubbornness—your silly, missish attitude?"

"I—"

The dowager let out a long breath and slumped, the angry color leaving her face. A tear ran down her cheek into a deep furrow that ran to the corner of her drooping mouth. Her wrinkled, sagging skin seemed to hang loosely on the underlying bones, and the gray, unhealthy color alarmed Hannah.

She moved over to sit on the edge of the bed and grasp the dowager's left hand in her own.

"Is it truly too much to ask?" Lady Blackwold murmured. "All I want is to see my Henry—and you— happy. Will you not consider it?"

"I don't—"

The dowager shook her head. "I am as bad as an old fishwife." A harsh laugh broke from her. "I am not so foolish that I do not realize it. But there are so few ways I can help anyone anymore, and I worry so about Henry. And you, my dear. You are a young woman, alone in an essentially foreign land. Have you truly considered what that entails? I am not a wealthy woman, Miss Cowles. In the end, I can give Henry nothing. Surely, you understand? Blackwold has everything, and Georgina will marry well, I am sure of it. Carter, well," she shrugged, "he has his living. And you—you may be an heiress, but there are dozens of wealthy women who lead unhappy lives—unaccepted by Society, despite their money. Can you not ease my mind that both you and Henry will both be taken care of? Life could be so pleasant for you both, and Henry could obtain the title and estate he so deserves. Will you not give me your promise, so I can go to my rest with peace of mind?"

"I wish I could." Hannah shook her head and stood to look out the window.

The sky was still clear blue and dotted with fluffy clouds, but despite the sunny, calm weather, her low spirits saw touches of gray in the clouds, a darkening on their undersides, threatening a storm.

"Have you not wanted a home of your own? A place where you belong and can call your own?"

The dowager's question pierced Hannah's heart like an arrow from a British longbowman. *Yes. I have always wanted my own home.* It was why she'd come to England. So why did her very soul resist the notion so fiercely now?

Blackwold... A small voice within her cried.

He had a home—and it was not hers.

"Miss Cowles?" The dowager prompted her when Hannah remained in front of the window, silently staring out over the lawn to the cliffs and the vast expanse of sky beyond.

"I..." Hannah straightened. She refused to allow herself to sink into a maudlin sensibility that would only lead to weeping and tearing of hair. "I will consider your request."

"Promise me. Please." The dowager leaned toward her, one hand outstretched.

"I promise to consider it." Hannah turned with a smile, though it felt pasted onto her stiff lips. "You cannot ask for more."

"Matters must be settled before I die."

Her smile turned into a laugh. "You will not die so soon, I assure you." She picked up *The Castle of Otranto* and waved it in the air. "Are you sure you don't wish to know Theodore's fate?"

The dowager shook her head in resignation, though some of the tension tightening her features melted away. She grinned and rolled her eyes heavenward. "I suppose it is the best you can do, so read on. Let us see what befalls Theodore and hope whatever fate overtakes him, it will put him out of his misery."

"I can't guarantee it—he seems to go from one terrible circumstance to a worse one."

"Then let us hope he dies soon so we can order another book." The dowager laughed. "You see, Miss Cowles? I am feeling better already since your promise, lukewarm though it may have been."

"I'm glad of it." Hannah seated herself and opened the book at the small bit of paper she'd used to mark their place.

Lady Blackwold leaned back against her pile of pillows and folded her hands over the covers. "Henry will be pleased," she murmured as Hannah began to read.

A headache pierced her temple at the words, but Hannah ignored the pain and began to read. Further argument seemed pointless.

Perhaps by tomorrow, the dowager would have forgotten all about her ridiculous notion to marry her grandson off to Hannah.

Chapter Fifteen

By three that afternoon, Lady Blackwold was nodding off, so Hannah left her in peace and wandered down to the small sitting room next to the library on the ground floor. To her surprise, both Gina and Blackwold were there, along with Mr. Carter Hodges and a young man Hannah had never seen before.

Shifting from one foot to the other, the stranger stood near the rose velvet-draped windows, his shoulders stooped as if he were embarrassed by his extraordinary height. It might have only been because he was also very thin, but he seemed to tower above everyone, including Blackwold, by several inches. His black hair was cut neatly and brushed back from his high forehead, and a pair of round glasses made it difficult to see the color of his eyes. The glasses flashed in the sunlight from the window as he kept glancing at Gina, who stood nearby, flushed and occasionally looking up at him.

When her gaze caught his, Gina's blush deepened. A smile danced over her mouth, creating appealing dimples in her rounded cheeks.

Grinning, Hannah entered the room. "I didn't realize we had guests. I hope I am not intruding."

"Come in, Miss Cowles." Blackwold turned to her. His face relaxed as if her arrival brought him a great deal of relief. He gestured toward his uncle. "Uncle Carter heard that Lady Blackwold is ill and came to offer her support. Brought his new curate, Mr. Furlong, as well. Miss Cowles, Mr. Furlong." He made the introductions hurriedly before pulling out his pocket watch and flipping it open.

The tall, thin gentleman hurriedly sketched a bow, his eyes blinking rapidly behind his glasses. "Miss Cowles," he murmured. Then, as if he couldn't help himself, he looked again at Gina.

Her smile widened, her dimples deepening, and she flushed again before clasping her hands demurely at her waist and fixing her gaze on his feet.

Oh, dear. Curates were not renowned for their great wealth. Hannah could just imagine what Lady Blackwold would say. She couldn't control a small twinge.

She glanced at Blackwold to see if he'd noticed the burgeoning attraction between Gina and the curate. He seemed to sense her stare and looked at her. A small V of concern burrowed between his brows. His brown eyes, instead of being cold with anger, seemed to be filled with deep sadness, which struck her as worse.

If Gina did her duty as expected, unhappiness seemed inevitable unless they traveled to London for her Season too quickly for her to fall in love with Mr. Furlong as she threatened to do.

Instead of watching his young curate, Mr. Hodges had fixed his attention upon Hannah. "How is my mother's health?" he asked with his abrupt cadence.

"She is doing very well, I believe." Her gaze drifted from the vicar to Blackwold. His attention had wandered, and he was staring out of the window with an abstracted air. "Though of course, I am no physician."

"My nephew reported that you have been reading to her in the afternoons. That is very considerate of you," the vicar said.

"It is a pleasure," Hannah murmured.

"Do you appreciate gardens, Mr. Furlong?" Gina asked. She peeped up at him out of the corner of her eye, smiled, and made a brief gesture at the door.

"Yes, indeed, Miss Hodges. I am a great student of nature," he replied with such enthusiasm that his long limbs twitched and seemed to move of their own accord toward the door.

"Some of our bulbs are already blooming—I noticed it the other day. Would you like to see them? Their perfume is wonderful. When I walked by one bed this morning, their delicious fragrance absolutely filled the air." Gina took two quick steps past Blackwold. Her lovely eyes were bright with excitement, and her cheeks glowed a rosy pink.

"If we have your permission, Lord Blackwold?" The curate bowed to him and then turned to Mr. Hodges. "And if it is acceptable, Mr. Hodges?"

Annoyance tightened the skin around the vicar's eyes and mouth, and Blackwold's emotionless face hinted that he wasn't best pleased, either, but he nodded.

"Fifteen minutes," Blackwold said. Then, as if aware that he sounded curt, he added, "Clouds are sweeping in from the ocean. Rain, I expect."

Gina's smile widened, and her brows rose as she gazed at her uncle Carter expectantly.

"Very well," the vicar said. "Fifteen minutes. I shall spend the time with my mother." He sounded like he was about to slam a gavel down and pronounce doom on all heretics.

Hannah bit the inside of her cheeks and stared at the rose-and-blue Oriental carpet while Gina and Mr. Furlong left the room in a flurry of swishing skirts and clatter of leather shoes.

"Before I attend to my mother, I have received a letter for you, Miss Cowles. My brother forwarded it. I gather it is from the bank manager." He pulled a thick envelope from his breast pocket and held it out, his gaze fixed on her. The wrinkles in the corners of his gray eyes revealed his curiosity, and his smug half-smile made her think that he believed whatever was in the missive was not good news.

"Thank you." She took the letter and held it reluctantly, unsure if she wanted to read it with an audience watching her reaction so closely.

Carter glanced at Blackwold and then the door. "I shall leave you, then." He gave a shallow bow and left, his back rigidly straight as he marched through the door.

When she looked at Blackwold, he was studying her with a slight frown.

Then an amused glint lit his brown eyes. "Miles Furlong," he said, watching her.

She raised a brow, thinking about Gina's comment that Blackwold was one of the mentally unstable Hodges. She shoved the thick missive into her pocket through the slit in the side of her skirt.

"Despite it, I doubt he will get very far," he said with a perfectly straight face, despite the impish light in his eyes.

Hiding a laugh behind one hand, she couldn't help a small snort of amusement. The curate's parents had been unusually cruel when naming their child. Or oblivious. Or perhaps they had hoped that he would, indeed, *go far*. Miles, in fact.

The laughter in his gaze faded as he watched her. In a mercurial change of mood, he asked, "And you remember nothing but a griffin ring? You saw neither the color of the jewels in its eyes nor the face of the man on the beach?"

She glanced over her shoulder and listened for the vicar's footsteps. A floorboard creaked and then she heard measured steps ascending the main staircase.

"No." She sighed and shrugged. "You've asked me that more times than I can remember, and my answer is always the same: no. I saw the ring and his hat. And greatcoat. A bit of the side of his face, perhaps, but not enough to recognize his features again. Indeed, for all I saw, it could have been you."

"It could have." He strode closer to the window and stared outside. "Ah. More visitors." He turned to her and smiled, though his eyes were sad. "You will be relieved to know that I doubt I shall ask you that particular question again."

"I don't know why you've persisted in asking it so many times as it is."

He chuckled, though he didn't sound amused. "No. I don't suppose you do."

Hannah studied him, trying to understand his strange mood. Unfortunately, before she could formulate a question, the butler threw open the drawing room door.

"Lady Northrop and Lady Alice Boynton, my lord," Hopwood announced, standing with his arm propping open the door to allow the passage of the ladies.

Lady Northrop swept into the room first, and Hannah's initial impression was one of exquisite taste and fashion. Her figure was as slim as a young woman's, and even her pale brown hair seemed untouched by gray, although she had to have been in her late thirties to have a daughter old enough to make her bow to Society.

Glancing around the room, Lady Northrop's blue eyes drifted over Hannah with all the recognition she showed to one of the Greek vases on pedestals framing the door. She smiled and moved forward, holding out her hand to Blackwold.

"It is so good to see you again, Lord Blackwold. We are grateful to you for your gracious invitation to break our journey here. Particularly as I understand your poor Grandmother's health is failing, and it is not the best time to receive visitors." Her gaze flickered briefly to Hannah.

"I'm sure she will be delighted to learn of your arrival." Blackwold's neutral voice and bow could hardly be called warmly welcoming.

Hannah forced herself to keep her gaze politely fixed on the women instead of studying Blackwold as she wanted to do. She had the distinct impression that Lady Northrop missed very little and would be unlikely to approve of any glances exchanged between Hannah and Blackwold.

A young woman, Lady Alice, moved to stand beside her mother, a vision in a pale pearl gray velvet traveling dress cut in severe lines that only made her seem more feminine. She was as slender and fine-boned as her mother, but where her mother's hair was light brown, hers was pale blonde. Two curls bobbed on either side of her heart-shaped face, beneath the graceful curve of her bonnet's brim, and traveling had tinged her cheeks a delicate pink.

"Lady Northrop and Lady Alice, may I present Miss Cowles, lately from Boston?" Blackwold said, performing the introductions in a careless way that made Hannah want to pinch his arm. His glance kept roving from the window to the door, for all the world as if planning his escape.

Well, she had no intention of allowing him to leave her here with these two women. Just as she'd taken an immediate liking to Gina, she had nothing but the coldest of feelings for both ladies standing in front of her, beautiful though they both may be. She'd met many such ladies in Boston, with their gracious, cutting manners and belief that the most valuable qualities to obtain consisted solely of social position, wealth, and of course, fashionableness.

Let's not forget good taste. One must have standards, after all.

She flashed a quick glance at Blackwold, taking in his unbuttoned waistcoat, rumpled jacket, and loose cravat. A warm smile curved her mouth as another rush of tenderness filled her. He looked so dear, and as she watched, his forelock fell over his brow, obscuring his left eye.

"It is lovely to make your acquaintance, Lady Northrop. Lady Alice." Hannah sketched a curtsey. "However, I should see if Lady Blackwold requires anything."

"She can ring." Blackwold frowned.

Hannah smiled. "Yes, but you know she is so kind that she hates to do so for fear of disturbing us. I look forward to seeing you tonight at supper." She looked at Lady Northrop. "If you will excuse me?"

"Certainly," Lady Northrop replied. Her lips curved upward, but the gracious expression failed to reach her cold eyes. "And we look forward to visiting the Dowager Lady Blackwold later, when she feels strong enough."

"I will let her know." Hannah picked up her skirts and escaped into the hallway.

Remembering that Carter Hodges was most likely still with his mother, Hannah decided to intrude upon Gina's idyll, instead.

Gina wouldn't thank her, but Hannah preferred her company to that of the vicar's. And she had to admit that she was curious about Miles Furlong.

Miles Furlong. She giggled, remembering the merry gleam in Blackwold's brown eyes when he divulged the curate's full name. *Really, how could his parents be so reprehensible as to name their child Miles when they had a surname of Furlong?*

And why is it that Blackwold can always make me laugh?

Chapter Sixteen

Moving quickly, Hannah went out into the garden. Gina had been correct to praise the flower beds. A few bulbs had begun blooming in February, and early daffodils and crocuses were almost at the end of their cycle. However, there were a few varieties still blooming, as well as hyacinths, tulips, and a few other flowers, giving the garden the appeal of a sheltered green bower interwoven with rich yellow, blue, red, and white strands of color. As soon as she stepped into the brisk air, she took a deep breath. The scent was so powerful that she seemed to be entirely bathed in flowers. A smile of pleasure settled over her face.

The scent of spring. She stooped to touch a late daffodil. The bright yellow trumpet released its heady scent at her touch, but she resisted the urge to pick it. Daffodils had always been her favorite flower. Yellow was such a sunny, cheerful color, and their fragrance raised her mood further. She thought she'd never been so completely happy before.

When she moved, the thick letter in her pocket rustled. Her stomach tightened.

Might as well read it and get it over with, whatever it is. She let out a long breath. Most likely, it was a simple confirmation of the transfer of her funds to the Bank of England, she thought, trying to recapture her previous euphoria.

She reached in and pulled the documents out, breaking the red wax seal of the covering note. One piece of paper had been folded around another letter with a different seal. She smoothed open the first sheet and skimmed down to the signature: *Captain Brian Hodges.* The note was brief, written in bold, masculine handwriting.

Dear Miss Cowles,

The bank manager of the Bank of England, Mr. Herbert Greene, has entrusted the enclosed correspondence to me. We felt it best to send it to you as expeditiously as possible. Mr. Greene expressed profound concern for your account and the state of your fortunes, and he will be pleased to discuss the matter with you at your earliest convenience.

The enclosed correspondence was sent to you, in care of Mr. Greene, by a Mr. Winthrop of Boston in the United States of America. He is, I believe, the lawyer entrusted with the management of your father's estate.

We hope the missive serves to bring clarity to what appears to be a difficult situation.

My brother, Mr. Carter Hodges, has expressed himself willing to forward any correspondence you may care to send to either Mr. Greene or your willing servant.

With sincerest regards,

Brian Hodges

The sick feeling in the pit of her stomach hardened. The palms of her hands grew damp and her icy fingers shook as she broke the seal on the second letter. The precise, copperplate signature at the bottom was indeed her lawyer's: *James Winthrop.*

His beautifully regular writing almost filled the page, and her gaze drifted past the greeting and what seemed like an entire first paragraph of apologies. *I dislike writing you about such a matter... find myself in an extremely difficult position... messenger disappeared... authorities have been unable to locate either him or your funds... misappropriated...*

Theft...

Line after line of Winthrop's cursive writing, detailing how Hannah's inheritance had vanished somewhere between Boston and London; stolen by the courier sent with it to ensure its safe arrival at the Bank of England.

The blue sky swirled dizzily around her. She sat down with a thud on the low stone wall, edging the terrace. *Gone.* Her inheritance was gone—or as good as. Certainly, if she'd had her way, it would all have been gone. She had to be at least a little grateful to Mr. Winthrop for convincing her to keep back some of her funds—not send it all to England.

However, what he'd kept in reserve was a tiny amount. The income from it would provide her less than three hundred dollars a year—what was that in pounds? She had no idea. Not enough, certainly, to hire servants or live like a lady.

Was it enough to stay in England at all?

Her cold fingers pressed against her mouth.

Even if she went to London with Gina, what could she truly hope for? She had nothing—she was not an heiress after all. In near panic, her thoughts whirled to Henry Hodges. He might be her last chance—what of his proposal? It was likely to be the only one she'd ever get, now. Would he withdraw it if he knew?

There was still the possibility of her father's title. There might even be some income from whatever estates were attached to it. Assuming the dowager's notion of having Hannah's husband apply for the title even worked.

Strange how she suddenly found Henry not so dreadful, after all. The iron bands squeezing her heart tightened further. She wasn't attracted to him, but he might be her last chance for marriage and a home of her own.

Or could she bring herself to face a life one step away from poverty? Other women had been forced to do so. Perhaps she could find some kind of employment. Become a companion like her beloved Mrs. Lawrence.

She remembered the letters Mrs. Lawrence had preserved in her small box. They'd been from her husband—personal and with small touches of humor. Nothing terribly romantic or exciting, and yet they'd revealed the deep connection between the two, a sense of shared interests and cherished love.

Hannah had loved her, as well, like her own mother. She'd tried to treat her as one of the family, but she was well aware that no matter how comfortable she thought they all were, Mrs. Lawrence never forgot that she was a paid companion. She was always a bit apart, a touch reserved, and her employment was not a situation one would accept unless one had no choice.

However, it was an alternative. She could offer to be a companion to the dowager...

What if the dowager didn't want—or need—a companion? What would happen if she refused to marry Henry, and they asked her to leave? Where would she go? How would she live with no money?

She'd have to sell her jewelry—that much was certain. That would provide her with enough to live on for a while.

Or she could return to Boston. That would please Mr. Winthrop, and it would keep whatever was left of her fortune from the risk of another transfer. All-in-all, that was the most practical solution. Sell her jewelry, buy a ticket on the next packet out of Liverpool, and return to a lonely life in Boston.

Feeling numb, she got up and walked across the terrace to the shallow flagstone steps, edged with jonquils and narcissus. She barely saw the flowers, barely noticed their heady fragrance as she stepped down onto the path that led through the herb garden to the rose beds. A splash of pink caught her attention. Yesterday, she'd noticed that one rose, Old Blush, had buds preparing to open.

She straightened and took a deep breath as she folded the letters together and shoved them back through the slit into her pocket. A decision could wait—would have to wait. Looking around, she saw that the paths were deserted and showed no signs of footprints.

Thinking that Gina might have led Mr. Furlong—*Miles Furlong, indeed*, she smiled although her lips felt stiff—to the rougher area near the cliff trail, she started off in that direction.

However, as she moved down the path, a flicker of white against the brown and green fields made her look that way. Gina and Mr. Furlong had left the gardens proper and were, indeed, in the wilder area between the grounds of the house and the cliffs. She picked up her skirts and walked toward them, her curiosity getting the better of her.

Gina and Mr. Furlong weren't standing, enjoying the view. They were on their hands and knees, their bottoms in the air and their noses almost touching the rough grass.

As if hearing her steps, Gina raised her head and looked over her shoulder. "Hannah! Oh, do come and see what Mr. Furlong is showing me. I had no idea there was such a variety of life in even the smallest square. Why, it is like one of our cities in miniature, with tiny insects rushing about their daily errands. And there is a lovely spider—you must look through Miles's magnifying glass, the markings are exquisite!"

Miles? Dismay tightened the back of Hannah's already tense neck. So, Gina felt comfortable using Mr. Furlong's first name, so soon after their first meeting. They had only been alone together for a few minutes. Surely, that was a hint that an unusual level of intimacy had grown between the two far too quickly for good sense or comfort.

Miles sat back on his heels and held out a large magnifying glass with a brass handle. "Do you wish to observe, Miss Cowles?" The expectant expression on his face gave no suggestion that he'd noticed anything amiss in Gina's use of his first name.

The two seemed quite companionable and content with each other's company. In fact, to Hannah's increasing alarm, Gina didn't seem to be pretending an interest in ants and spiders and whatever else she was looking at. She actually seemed to find the creatures as fascinating as Miles Furlong did.

Worse and worse. The identical, hopeful expressions on their faces as they glanced up at Hannah reminded her precisely of Mrs. Lawrence's letters and the harmony of expression she'd seen in her parents' faces when they'd been pouring over maps. Such accord was a rare and precious thing and could only mean a great many tears when Gina eventually went to London.

"Hannah?" Gina asked again, placing her fingers under Miles's wrist to push his hand and the magnifying glass another inch closer to Hannah.

"No." She took a step back. While she wasn't frightened of spiders, neither did she want to examine them nose-to-nose. Or beak-to-nose, or whatever spiders had in the middle of their faces. "That is, I don't wish to interrupt, and I forgot my shawl." She rubbed her arms, her mood brittle and unsure. "I simply came outside for a breath of fresh air."

"Oh." Gina's face fell, and she glanced at Miles for support. "Are you sure you don't want to look, Hannah? It truly is fascinating."

"I'm sure it is."

"We noticed that other visitors have arrived," Miles said, handing the magnifying glass to Gina when Hannah refused to take it. An anxious look tightened the skin over his sharp cheekbones. "Is Mr. Hodges requesting our attendance? Should we return to the house?"

Gina flashed an angry look over her shoulder at the manor. "My uncle can wait a few more minutes. I want to see if that pretty spider catches her supper."

"Lady Northrop and her daughter have arrived," Hannah replied, trying not to think about some poor, helpless insect, caught and eaten by a spider.

It probably won't feel any worse than I do right now, drained of everything.

"Oh." Gina snorted and turned back, her gaze searching the ground in front of her. "Blackwold's betrothed—or nearly betrothed. They will have tea and gossip and not miss us in the least. We should have another half-hour before they even realize we are not in the room with them." She turned her head to give Miles a quick, sweet smile.

He smiled back, his blue eyes softening behind the round lenses of his glasses. "Mr. Hodges—"

"Uncle Carter will never miss your presence, Miles, I assure you," Gina said, interrupting him and leaning down to peer through the magnifying glass.

He gave another uneasy glance at the house and then bent over again, his long fingers gently moving blades of grass aside to improve Gina's view of whatever creature was living down there.

Hannah studied their bent backs and shoulders brushing as they examined life in miniature on the rough ground. She sighed. "I'm returning to the house."

Neither one of them appeared to hear her. Miles murmured something in a soft voice to Gina. She giggled and leaned closer to him, moving the glass a fraction in his direction.

"Goodbye," Hannah said. "I'm going to jump off the cliff."

Gina flapped a hand over her shoulder.

"If I survive, I'm going to go tell Lady Northrop and Lady Alice exactly what I think of them," Hannah added. It was perfectly clear that no one was interested in anything she had to say.

Gina's wave became a definite shooing-away gesture.

"Miss Cowles!" Henry Hodges suddenly appeared a few yards away. Although he cast one supercilious glance at the only visible part of the pair on the ground—their bottoms— he failed to display either puzzlement or concern over their extraordinary behavior. If anything, his gray eyes sparkled as if he were excited. "I am delighted to see you." He held out his crooked arm.

Another deep breath whispered over her lips. With a sense of resignation, she slipped her hand through the crook of his arm, and they began to walk back to the house. Her stomach gurgled. Should she tell him about the loss of her fortune?

"Have you met Lady Northrop and her daughter, Lady Alice?" he enquired with a smile. The brilliance of his eyes increased as did his pace until he was almost dragging her across the uneven ground. "Blackwold is exceedingly fortunate—Lady Alice is a lovely young woman. Fresh and innocent as a summer morning."

And rich. Let's not forget that. Her jaw and her grip on his arm tightened a moment as she murmured a vague agreement, her sick feeling returning full force.

"You are very similar—both lovely women—she the new morn while you are a riper, mature summer. She is so fair, and you must have noticed her blue eyes, as translucent as the clear sky. Though yours are as dark as the ocean, and your hair the color of honey." It was clear—at least to Hannah—that he preferred the new dawn over ripe noon, though he tried to sound just as enthusiastic when he remembered to praise her.

Her facial muscles ached as they grew tighter and tighter over her forehead and around her mouth. Lady Alice was eighteen, only two years younger than Hannah, and the same age as Gina. Hardly a vast difference, even if she did feel like a middle-aged aunt at times around Gina.

"Are you staying for supper?" Hannah asked, trying to change the subject of conversation.

"Yes. Uncle Carter has even managed to convince Grandmother to join us, so we shall have quite a pleasant party."

Pleasant wasn't the adjective that leapt to Hannah's mind, though perhaps with Lady Northrop present, the dowager would manage to be a little less acerbic.

Or perhaps not.

What would the dowager say when she learned that Hannah was as poor as Mr. Hodges's young curate? It didn't bear consideration.

Henry dragged her even faster up the terrace steps toward the door. "And Grandmother mentioned that you were quite pleased when she mentioned my proposal." With his free hand, he pressed her fingers into the crook of his arm.

"I am considering it," she replied sharply. The last thing she wanted to do was to discuss it now.

"That is all I ask, Miss Cowles." He held the door open for her. "I am sure that the advantages will become apparent upon consideration."

Even to a woman as dull as I am? Or as poor as I am? Blackwold was right—I should have drowned like a proper British lady, then I wouldn't be facing such a bleak future. She mumbled a response that could be taken as agreement if one didn't listen too closely.

It seemed to satisfy Henry. His smile grew as he led the way to the drawing room. He paused at that doorway, clearly forgetting her until she swept past him, her skirts brushing his leg.

She entered an empty room.

Or nearly empty. Hopwood was leaning over the low table in front of the fireplace, collecting half-empty teacups and plates and placing them on a tray.

He glanced up and straightened when Hannah and Henry entered the room. "Lord Blackwold and his guests have retired to their rooms to prepare for dinner, sir." He bowed. "Miss Cowles." He folded his hands over his plump stomach and awaited their orders.

"I shall retire as well, then," Hannah said, grasping the excuse to flee to her room and collect herself. The corners of the letter kept poking through the thin linen of her pocket, reminding her that at some point, she was going to have to admit that she was not the wealthy heiress that she'd claimed.

She'd always thought of herself as a calm and thoroughly self-sufficient woman, but somehow, the past few hours had pushed her off balance. Now, she felt like a top wobbling near the edge of the table. She needed to collect herself before facing Lady Northrop and the dowager at supper.

And she needed to see if she had anything in her trunk that she could salvage. Lady Blackwold's old, remade gowns were not going to be sufficient for her last appearance as an heiress.

One final night, and then she'd have to decide in which direction to take her future.

Chapter Seventeen

When Hannah began pulling dresses out of her salt-encrusted trunk, she found the fitted, fringed buckskin jacket her mother had specially made to match the frontiersman jacket her husband had obtained from a trapper. Hannah gently removed it and laid it on the bed, the heaviness in her chest making it difficult to breathe.

Even her limbs seemed uncoordinated and strapped with weights as she moved to hold the jacket up to her in front of the mirror. Her eyes burned with hot tears.

Several years had passed since her mother died, and yet at times, the wounds seemed as fresh as ever. She ached with a deep, tearing loss for both of her parents. How she missed their laughter and optimism, and most of all, their arms around her shoulders. A tear trickled over her cheek, and she brushed it away with the back of her hand.

Her mother and father never let the snobbery of others worry them. Her hand smoothed over the soft buckskin. In fact, they'd taken to wearing their matching fringed jackets when visiting friends, as if to proclaim that they were simple Americans with no interest in titles, peerages, and estates.

Hannah's gaze lingered on the fringes. Her parents were not the first to do such a thing. Benjamin Franklin had worn a simple fur hat while acting as a diplomat in France, in a clever attempt to appear as an unsophisticated frontiersman. The United States of America had subsequently profited from the sophisticated Parisians' low expectations of Mr. Franklin, unaware that he was a brilliant scientist and intellectual, definitely not the humble, uneducated backwoodsman he appeared to be.

Perhaps she ought to take a leaf from Mr. Franklin's book. Time and time again, it had been pointed out to Hannah that she had already failed to behave as a proper British lady, and indeed, she was not. Nor would she ever be. She glanced out the window at the flaming sunset. Her emotions threatened to rip her apart.

While she hadn't even been at Blackrock for a complete month, she felt at home. Her heart had soared when she'd watched the breathtaking view of the sun setting over the ocean, or the massive power of the clouds darkening to rage in a brief storm that ended in misty sunshine and the occasional distant rainbow. It would be painful to leave Blackrock Manor now, when she was just learning to appreciate its wild changes of mood.

She pulled out the letters and tucked them behind the secret panel of her trunk. What should she do? Did she have any hope of rebuilding her fortune? She had no idea what condition her father's abandoned estate was in, or if she'd even want to refurbish it and live there, if that was possible with her terribly reduced inheritance.

Would it be worthwhile? What if she didn't feel at home there as she did here?

But she'd come to England to make her home. She thought she belonged here, would fit in as she had not in Boston, where her parents had rented a humble apartment before one after the other had died. The epitaph in Boscastle would have served them just as well.

Hope, darkly tinged with bitterness, fluttered inside her. The dowager's request offered a way to fit in—a sure way to marry and settle down to start her own family, even without her own money. Perhaps she'd been foolish to think she could find love and happiness such as her parents had experienced. Their life had not been a perfect idyll, either. There were often times when her mother and father had fought—their words ringing with anger. There were difficulties, certainly, and times when Hannah had gone to bed and pressed the pillow over her ears, so she wouldn't have to hear their deep-throated, furious words.

What should she do?

Coldness stiffened her hands. What if she married Henry, and he turned out to be the man on the beach? Could she live with him, knowing that?

In truth, could she live with any of the Hodges, knowing that one of them was a murderer?

163

But if she went with Gina to London, what was the best that she could hope for? Without any funds, there were very few men who would even give her a second glance. And she could not expect to return to Cornwall and Blackrock Manor.

Her heart seemed to shrink within her chest as she took a long, shuddering breath. It might already be too late for her to find what her parents had had. *Too late...* Much too late.

The truth was harsh and unkind. She'd already fallen in love, but it was with a man she could not hope to marry—might not even *want* to marry if she knew everything about him.

Ruined, indeed, but not in the ridiculous way the villagers gossiped about. She was ruined because her heart was already filled with the dear image of Blackwold, his shaggy hair hanging over his left eye, his neckcloth loose and hanging down on either side of his strong neck, and his waistcoat unbuttoned and rumpled as he slouched in the chair next to her bed at three in the morning, asking her impertinent questions.

A trembling sigh escaped her as she stared in the mirror. What should she do? What had she really hoped to find by coming to England? She would never fit in and could not hope to outshine ladies such as Lady Alice or even her fashionable mother, Lady Northrop. And the trip had cost her everything: Mrs. Lawrence had been drowned and Hannah had lost her inheritance.

She straightened and picked at the fringe of the soft buckskin. Maybe it was time to stop trying so desperately to be a proper British lady or a rich heiress. Honesty was called for.

Though tonight was not the night for buckskin. Or the truth. Her mouth twisted ruefully. She returned to the gowns she'd removed from the trunk and flung onto the bed. She'd been so pleased with them when she left Boston, but now they all seemed slightly old-fashioned after seeing the well-fitted and obviously expensive dresses the other ladies had worn for traveling. If Lady Alice's silvery-gray traveling outfit was any indication, she would have some exceptional evening gowns for her first—and obviously only—Season in London.

Why she even bothered to go was beyond Hannah, although perhaps it was necessary for her to be presented at Court and all of that folderol. It was one social necessity she was glad didn't exist in America. Her hand smoothed over the shimmering folds of a geranium-colored silk dress. If she married Henry—or anyone else for that matter—and he somehow managed to receive her father's title, would she be required to be presented at Court, too?

Another unforeseen complication, and one she didn't relish. No wonder her father had abandoned his home and title and started wandering the world. His special genius had somehow managed to amass another fortune, even without a title or social position. He just used his wits and his cheerful gift for making friends with anyone, regardless of age, position, or wealth.

Enough. She was becoming maudlin, a useless mood that she detested.

She picked up the geranium silk dress and held it against her. The gleaming reddish color brought out the rose in her cheeks and made her eyes a darker, richer blue. Not that Henry would admire that change. He appeared to prefer lighter, sky blue eyes, and apparently, his cousin cherished similar tastes as he was going to marry the lovely Lady Alice.

Brushing out the dress, Hannah glanced up when the door opened.

Mary entered briskly and eyed the mound of dresses on the bed. "I'm to assist you to dress for dinner." She picked up the dress on top of the pile and turned to the armoire, folding it efficiently and placing it on one of the shelves. "I've done altering a white satin gown, if you wish it."

"This silk might be more suitable." Hannah held up the gown for the maid's inspection.

"One of your own," Mary muttered, folding another gown and putting it away.

"Yes, well, I thought since I have it now..."

"The white satin has got blue velvet trim with matching silk flowers. It were one of her ladyship's favorites." Mary's controlled expression gave no hint of emotion, and she carefully avoided Hannah's gaze.

After her illness, Hannah had realized that the way to Mary's heart was to let her care for her, but there was a limit to how much care she desired. She pressed her lips together and gave her silk dress a light shake.

"Could you assist me with this gown? I fear saltwater may have stained the fabric. It would be a terrible shame if it were ruined before I ever got the chance to wear it."

Mary paused in folding the last of the gowns on the bed. She stared at the dress, a frown puckering her brow. "The white satin might do for tonight."

"But don't you think Lady Alice might wear white? I fear I will be cast into the shade by her."

Eyes flashing at the thought, Mary grunted and took the silk dress out of Hannah's hands. "A girl like her can't never hope to wear this color. Let me look it over. There'll be no sign of salt when I finish, I promise you."

"Thank you, Mary. I knew you would understand." Hannah watched the maid examine the gown, feeling a little guilty even though she'd won this round.

An hour later and finally dressed in her silk dress, Hannah hesitated only a moment before clasping her pearl necklace around her neck. The square neckline needed something to set it off, and the pearls were demure enough for any unmarried woman. The shoulders draped nicely and flowed into sleeves that were full and gathered at the elbows, where they then fitted smoothly down to the wrists. She picked up her white evening gloves and touched one of the curls hanging in front of her ears.

Mary had outdone herself in creating a new hairstyle for Hannah. The back was braided and wound into a knot on her crown, leaving small curls around her face that echoed the soft curl of the white feather of her pearl and silver filigree headdress.

"You looks beautiful, Miss." Mary stood back and clasped her hands together at her waist, studying Hannah with a critical eye. "No one can fault you."

"And the credit belongs solely to you." Hannah smoothed the front of her dress again. "There is no sign of any salt or staining."

"No, miss. Weren't none to worry over. That trunk of yours must have floated on the air to shore to keep out the seawater so well."

Hannah laughed. "Perhaps it did." She took a deep breath and smoothed her dress again. "Well, I suppose I should join the others."

"Yes, Miss." Mary stepped aside and opened the bedroom door.

The silence in the hallway suggested that the others had already gone downstairs to the sitting room next to the library. There was a pianoforte in the corner of the room and several comfortable sitting areas, so it was the room the dowager preferred to use when she ventured down to the ground floor. As Hannah descended, light feminine laughter floated up the staircase, and she could hear the click of a man's heels against the oak floorboards.

Her hands curled at her sides, but she was almost laughing at herself when she stepped off the last stair. There was absolutely no reason for her to be nervous. It didn't matter in the slightest if Lady Alice outshone her. Blackwold was nearly betrothed to her—his opinion no longer mattered—and she knew what Henry thought.

Her smile died as she approached the door. Another tinkling cascade of laughter escaped from the room, and she felt like an unwanted intruder. She hated being the last one to enter a room. One never felt as if one belonged and could never really join a group and catch up on the conversation. One was always out of step.

Another lilting stream of laughter, male and female mingling happily, rose through the air. That had to be Lady

Alice—it sounded too young and carefree to be her mother or the dowager. She could just imagine Henry and Blackwold clustered around the young woman, smiling down at her, sharing a witticism.

Hannah took a deep breath and braced herself. One last, unpleasant thought rushed through her as she stepped over the threshold. Even Henry preferred Lady Alice, the perfect British lady.

What if Hannah lost him, as well?

The thought was absurd. She didn't even want him. In fact, it would be a relief if he eloped with Lady Alice, and she never saw either of them again. She forced a pleasant smile, raised her chin, and walked straight over to stand near the dowager's wing chair by the fire.

Looking around, she saw Gina and the three men, Blackwold, Henry, and the vicar, standing in an arc around Lady Alice. Her first reaction upon seeing her was relief that she hadn't worn the white dress with the blue trim. Gina was wearing a lovely white gown with trim of green leaves intertwined with yellow roses, and Lady Alice was wearing a pale ensemble that would have cast the dowager's remade dress into the shade.

Lady Alice's gown of *gros de Naples* was the palest pink imaginable, barely pink at all, with an overdress of sheer white silk gauze. The bodice was rather high in the front, but lower on the shoulders, emphasizing the lovely curve of her neck, shoulders, and hint of a bosom. The neckline was trimmed with a notched *ruche* of *gros de Naples* and the sleeves were short and extremely full, set in with a satin-corded band and long white *crèpe lisse* sleeves inserted at the shoulder. The elegant sleeves were confined at the wrists with broad seed-pearl bracelets.

Her jewelry consisted of a simple gold locket and small pearl earrings, and Hannah eyed the locket while fingering her own necklace. The pearls felt huge and ostentatious as she rubbed them and then touched her dangling earrings. Even her headdress felt too much. A simple pale pink ribbon had been threaded through the soft curls piled up on top of Lady Alice's head. She looked very young—fresh and appealing—and Hannah could see why Henry admired her.

In fact, she could see why all the men admired her. Even Gina appeared a trifle gauche, though her dress was fashionable and lovely on her, with a simple yellow ribbon threaded through her brown hair. She was clearly drinking in the elegance of Lady Alice's costume and probably making notes about modifications she might make to her own wardrobe.

Lady Northrop, sitting on the couch across from the dowager, flicked satisfied glances at her daughter, clearly pleased with the girl's reception. The older woman obviously spent time on her own toilet as well, for she wore a lovely blue silk gown fitted tightly on the bodice with drooping shoulders similar to her daughter's dress, but cut slightly higher and not quite as revealing. Her sleeves ballooned out from the shoulders to the elbows, where they were nipped in and fitted to the wrist.

Unlike her daughter's modest jewelry, the diamond collar necklace, set with deep blue sapphires, sparkled around her long neck, and diamond-and-sapphire earrings dangled from her small ears. Diamonds nestled amongst the curls and elaborate intertwined braids of her brown hair crowning her, and the jewels glittered like tiny stars as she moved her head.

Even the dowager, arising from her sickbed to entertain her guests, had made an obvious effort to dress well. Her black dress shimmered with the light cast by the fire, revealing the fabric to be a heavy and extremely expensive silk. Her gray hair was pinned up in curls around her face, and a lace-edged cap sat on top, with white silk ribbons fluttering down to the nape of her neck. Her jewelry consisted mostly of jet, but the darkness was enlivened by the thick ruffles of silver lace running around the high neckline of her gown and around the cuffs of her long sleeves.

She was flushed and grinning, breaking into a jolly laugh at some remark of Lady Northrop's before she noticed Hannah standing nearby. "Miss Cowles—there you are at last."

Hannah smiled, trying not to blush at the implication that she was the last one to arrive and therefore late.

"Join us." The dowager waved at the couch where Lady Northrop was sitting.

Although there was room next to her, Hannah really didn't want to sit so close. But it would be rude to move another chair into the gap between the two women, so she resigned herself and smiled. Her face was growing numb with the effort to retain her pleasant expression when she finally took the indicated seat.

Lady Northrop moved over a fraction, but her violet perfume filled the surrounding air. Her sharp elbow kept brushing Hannah's arm as she resumed her conversation with the dowager. "I truly do not want to live on Upper Seymour Street; I would much prefer Berkley Square. But thus far, we have simply been unable to locate any available apartments. This is Lady Alice's first," she smiled complacently and clasped her hands in her lap, "and if we are fortunate, *only* Season, so it must be perfection itself."

The dowager laughed. "I am sure she will make do, regardless of the address, and that is hardly a poor situation."

"Make do?" Lady Northrop murmured, her nose wrinkling as a look of distaste crossed her face. "We must certainly do better than that."

"Well, Blackwold has a townhouse on Portman Square, just around the corner, so perhaps Lady Alice might find it convenient, after all."

Lady Northrop sighed. "I suppose so. All these small matters are so tiresome." She pressed her fingertips to her temple for an instant. "I suppose I worry over nothing." A set, polite smile stretched her mouth as she turned to Hannah. "I understand you will be joining Miss Hodges in London, Miss Cowles. You must be very pleased."

"Yes, Miss Cowles is quite the American heiress," the dowager said before Hannah could reply.

She felt her cheeks flame, and she dropped her gaze to her clasped hands. The last thing she wanted to do was to admit the truth now, with Lady Northrop's critical gaze fixed on her. "That was my original plan," she said finally. Her fingers tightened. "To be honest, since the shipwreck, I have not had sufficient time to consider how I should proceed."

"Oh, yes. The wreck." Lady Northrop's voice sounded cold. "So unfortunate."

"Yes." Hannah could entirely agree with that statement: *Orion*'s sinking was unfortunate. At the very least.

"It is just too bad that you cannot join the girls at Almack's." Gazing at her fixedly, Lady Northrop's lips curved into a self-satisfied smile. "But of course, foreigners and the *nouveau riche* cannot hope to be granted entrance."

"I am hardly *nouveau riche*—my father was a baron."

"Would have been a baron," Lady Northrop corrected, her tight little smile never leaving her face. "According to Lady Blackwold, he never applied for the title, my dear. He as good as abandoned it, as well as his estates, when he left England. Hardly an illustrious background that would grant you entrance to such an exclusive gathering as the Wednesday night subscription ball at Almack's." She reached over her lap with her left hand and patted Hannah's knotted fingers. "You do have our sympathy, my dear. It must be terribly frustrating, but it cannot be helped. Nonetheless, you may find that you have no need to attend such functions if what I gather from Lady Blackwold's hints is true." Her blue eyes gleamed with curiosity.

Hannah glanced at the dowager. The elderly lady had a crafty grin as she winked at her.

"We shall see," Hannah said. *Just go ahead and tell her—I'm as poor as Mr. Furlong—maybe poorer. It's the honest answer.* But she could hardly believe it herself, much less admit it to the two women watching her like scavenging crows waiting for any sign of weakness. She forced herself to smile and loosen her clasped hands.

Thankfully, Mr. Hopwood stepped through the doorway at that moment and announced that dinner was served. The guests immediately rose and arranged themselves according to social position, leaving Mr. Furlong to escort Hannah as the least important people in the room.

Nothing like having your nose rubbed in it, Hannah thought wryly as they trailed into the dining room.

While excellent food was served, including a lovely lamb roast, crispy new potatoes, huge platters of delectable fish in a rich cream sauce, and several vegetable dishes, the conversation seemed to center upon London. Hannah had little to contribute.

She felt increasingly out of step and alone as she picked at a pickled cucumber and pushed it to the edge of her plate. The smell of vinegar made her choke. Even the men were caught up in discussions about some place called Tattersalls, horses, Hyde Park, and occasionally, places of interest to the ladies.

Gina and Lady Alice professed themselves to be fascinated and listened with wide-eyed eagerness while Hannah fought back yawns and the desire to return to the quiet of her room.

She needed to think.

More and more, she wondered if she truly should give up and return home, to assess the state of her finances. She did have at least one friend in Boston, Mrs. Pernell. She'd kindly offered Hannah a place to stay anytime she needed one, and since she was widowed, Hannah wouldn't be intruding on a large and busy household.

Of course, there was the matter of buying passage home.

Her head throbbed. She was relieved when the footman collected her plate and began serving the final course.

All she had to do was to get through dessert, spend five minutes with the dowager in the drawing room, and then give her excuses.

Chapter Eighteen

Unfortunately for Hannah, her plans to spend the evening in her room were upset by Lady Alice, who fastened on her the moment they stepped into the drawing room after dinner.

Touching her arm gently, Lady Alice drew Hannah aside. The other ladies went to the cluster of chairs near the fireplace, engrossed in a serious discussion about descending waistlines and the increasing width of skirts.

"I wanted to speak with you, Miss Cowles," Lady Alice said in a rushed voice, glancing at her seated mother. "I was not as kind to you as I ought to have been—even our dear Mr. Hodges noted it—and I must offer you my apologies. I do so want us to be friends. I confess that I was nervous about traveling to London, even with Miss Hodges. We three must help each other—do you not agree?" Her blue eyes searched Hannah's face eagerly.

When Hannah looked at her, she noticed the signs of worry and nervousness in the pinched skin between her fair brows and her constant biting of her plump lower lip.

Hannah nodded. "Yes—it is always best to be friends." A sigh almost escaped her at the thought. She didn't want to like Lady Alice—she preferred to think of her as a featherbrained snob, not as a nervous young woman anticipating her first Season in London.

"Thank goodness. I *knew* you would agree. You have such a kind face—even my dear Georgina said that you were simply the kindest woman imaginable." She linked arms with Hannah and drew her over to a pair of padded chairs near the pianoforte in the corner. "I was completely overcome with nerves when my mother informed me that we would be stopping our journey here for a few days. I have only met Lord Blackwold a few times, and never to talk to him. And even though my mother assures me that he is quite amiable—for a man—I was nearly prostrate when we arrived." Her eyes flickered in the direction of the door, clearly anticipating the arrival of the men.

"You didn't look at all nervous," Hannah assured her with a smile. "And Lord Blackwold appears to be quite friendly. I'm sure you have nothing to fear."

She giggled and hastily covered her mouth with her hand, her gaze straying again to the door. "Yes. And once we are married, I am sure I can manage him to be more to my liking." She broke off with a tiny laugh. "The first thing shall be his hair—I shall insist on it being properly trimmed and groomed. Why, he looks quite like one of those shaggy dogs one sees on farms. And I shall speak to his valet—he must either tidy Lord Blackwold's wardrobe, or I shall insist that he be let go and a valet hired who will ensure Lord Blackwold's neat appearance. I cannot bear to see him so rumpled and coarse. Why, if I did not know better, I would believe he was one of those wretched souls one sees wandering the streets, sleeping in alleyways and such." She gave a delicate shiver. "Why anyone should wish to sleep in an alleyway is beyond comprehension."

"I don't believe they wish to do so." Hannah's thoughts spun in circles. *She intends to change Blackwold—remake him into a different man.* How could she even consider such a thing? Blackwold was so endearing—so comfortable—just the way he was.

"Then why do they do it?"

"Why does who do what?" she asked in confusion.

"Those men—why do they sleep in alleyways if they do not wish to do so?"

"I think it is because they do not have the means to sleep anywhere else. They are poor."

"Is that truly the reason?" Lady Alice seemed surprised. "I had not realized it—though one does wonder."

"I suppose so." One wondered only if one decided to remain ignorant of the lives of those less fortunate. Some of the friendship she'd been experiencing for Lady Alice withered. She studied Lady Alice's pretty, young face. "Perhaps after you are married, you will decide that you prefer Lord Blackwold just as he is."

Lady Alice laughed and shook her head, her blonde curls bouncing. "Oh, no—he must be managed—that much is certain." Her gaze drifted to the door again. "If only he were more like his cousin, Mr. Henry Hodges. *He* is already quite a perfect gentleman, do you not agree? He is so neat and tidy—I cannot imagine that even Beau Brummel himself would outshine Mr. Hodges." She leaned forward, pressing her right hand over Hannah's fingers. "Oh, do you think he might be prevailed upon to speak to Lord Blackwold? Perhaps he could lend him his valet!"

"I don't know," Hannah replied, shifting uncomfortably. "That is the sort of thing that should wait until after you are married, I believe." How anyone could prefer Henry Hodges to Lord Blackwold was beyond her ability to understand, but it filled her with a sense of dismay.

Lady Alice was on the verge of betrothal to the wrong man. And Gina was about to be torn away from someone she clearly admired.

What was wrong, here, that these families could countenance making so many tragic mistakes as a matter of course? Was this coldhearted decision-making the reason her own father had abandoned his country and his birthright?

The thought made her ill. She could imagine nothing but quiet misery for everyone at Blackrock Manor. Their fates seemed far worse than her own loss of her inheritance.

Oddly enough, that made her realize that she'd made a decision.

She would not marry Henry Hodges, even if he wanted to marry her after learning about her circumstances. And just as soon as she could arrange it, she was going to return to Boston.

The thought tore through her with a sense of loss. Her vision of having her own home, a place where she truly belonged, seemed further away than ever.

And Blackwold... What about him? Whatever would become of him and that silly lock of hair that kept falling into his eyes? A soft smile curved her mouth at the thought of smoothing it back from his forehead.

"Mama says she let go Papa's valet from his bachelor days and took Papa under such strict management that she has grown quite reconciled to being seen in Society with him. She says that it should be quite simple to perform the same service for Lord Blackwold."

"I'm afraid I don't know Lord Blackwold well enough to predict, Lady Alice," Hannah replied with a twinge of discomfort. She knew him well enough to know that it was highly unlikely that Lady Alice would find him an easy subject to manage if even his grandmother had given up.

"Of course." Lady Alice smiled happily, her eyes gazing dreamily past Hannah's shoulder, apparently lost in contemplation of the changes she might wreak on her betrothed. Then she sobered and caught Hannah's glance. "My apprehensions are ridiculous—I know they are—but I cannot seem to stop thinking about it, particularly at night. Mama says I am all in a flutter for nothing." She leaned forward and placed a hand on Hannah's arm. She could feel the chill of Lady Alice's fingers through her sleeve, revealing the young woman's nervousness more clearly than her impulsive words. "You are so calm—I wish I could be as placid as you are—even after everything that has happened to you. It must have been horribly frightening when the storm struck. I cannot swim, you see, and I am terribly afraid of ships. They creak so and bob around in the waves as if they would roll over at any moment. You are so brave—I can only admire you."

Hannah murmured a vague reply, unsure what to say. The experience was just as terrifying as Lady Alice imagined, but agreeing with her and elaborating on the tragedy was not something she was prepared to undertake.

"You are truly a heroine," Lady Alice concluded.

"Gina—that is, Georgina—says that you are an accomplished musician, Lady Alice. Do you enjoy playing the pianoforte?" Hannah gestured to the instrument nearby in hopes of changing the subject to something less personal, even if she had to ascribe words to Gina which the girl never said.

"Why, yes! I adore music!" Her eyes sparkled as she leapt to her feet. "Do you play, as well?"

Hannah shrugged. "I am an indifferent musician at best. What is your favorite piece?"

"Oh, I adore Haydn, particularly that sonata in F major—I much prefer cheerful pieces, do you not?"

"They are, indeed, pleasant," Hannah agreed as she moved to the small table next to the pianoforte, where a stack of music, both published and hand-written, lay. She rifled through them, finding one in what she suspected was Lady Blackwold's neat hand. "Here is a piece by Haydn in G major. Perhaps you would like to play it for us?"

"Oh, yes!" Lady Alice took the music and glanced at the pages, which had been folded together. "I adore this piece!"

With Hannah's assistance, Lady Alice opened the pianoforte and arranged the music in front of her before taking a seat on the bench. "Will you turn the page for me?"

"Certainly."

Just as Hannah took a position next to the instrument, the men filed into the room. Lady Northrop glanced at the doorway and then over to her daughter. Another satisfied smile crossed her face. Lady Alice was behaving perfectly. Her mother was clearly pleased with her daughter's decision to prove her musical skills and thereby, her good breeding.

Without any need for further cajoling, Lady Alice began playing, her fingers moving with delicate precision. She was, indeed, a competent musician, and the men smiled at the vision she presented, seated at the pianoforte, illuminated by softly glowing candles positioned on either side of her.

Henry moved to stand next to Hannah. With a smile and gesture, he indicated that he would turn the page of music for Lady Alice when required.

After catching Lady Alice's eye, Hannah retreated to her original chair. Carter Hodges had taken a seat in the padded chair Lady Alice had vacated, and Lord Blackwold stood near the fire. He propped one arm on the mantle and gazed at the flames, apparently absorbed in his own thoughts. Or the sprightly music.

"My daughter is an accomplished musician, is she not?" Lady Northrop asked him.

Lady Alice, distracted by Henry leaning closer, skipped a note. She recovered swiftly, though bright pink bloomed over her cheeks.

"Fortunately, I am tone deaf," Blackwold commented, his mouth twisting wryly. His gaze remained fixed on the flames crackling behind the embroidered fire screen.

Lady Northrop sucked in a sharp breath while the dowager snorted.

Glancing at Lady Alice, Hannah was relieved to see that the girl was so absorbed in the music that she missed Blackwold's comment.

"It is good to see you looking so well, Miss Cowles," the vicar said quietly. "We were all quite concerned when you survived the ordeal of the *Orion*'s wreck, only to fall ill."

"Thank you," Hannah replied. She kept her gaze focused on Lady Alice, hoping that the vicar would see that she preferred to listen to the music rather than converse. Why did everyone insist on questioning her about the tragedy? Why couldn't they find some other topic to gossip about? Surely, there were other scandals they could discuss.

"It must have been terrifying, seeing your fellow travelers bludgeoned to death."

She stiffened, cold as a daffodil encased in ice by a late winter's storm. Why did he use that word? How could he know they were bludgeoned—poor Officer Trent...

Her breath caught in her throat as she tried to remain calm. Her lips trembled. She forced a smile, her hands twisting together in her lap.

His voice... Could the vicar's clockwork voice be the one she'd heard, ordering a man to club Officer Trent to death? Could he be the murderer who caused the horrifying wreck?

"Miss Cowles!" Carter leaned closer to her, touching her clasped hands. "Are you well? You have grown fearfully pale—we cannot have you suffering a relapse."

Her gaze caught his. His gray eyes were alert with intelligence, watching her closely.

He knows! He knows that I saw him on the beach! The chill of that recognition pierced her to the bone, sending uncontrollable shivers through her body.

She swallowed once. Again. Forced her stiff neck to turn her head toward Lady Alice. *Breathe. Listen to the music. Smile.* Somehow, she remained seated with a polite smile fixed on her face, even though her mind echoed with screaming and the memory of the bodies in the swirling water around her.

"Miss Cowles?" Blackwold joined them, his brow furrowed. A lock of brown hair fell over his eye. Inconsequentially, she noticed his cravat was coming undone and there was a small spot of red wine, like fresh blood, staining it. "Are you unwell?"

She rose unsteadily. Blackwold's strong hand slipped under her elbow, bracing her before she toppled over into the vicar's lap. "Perhaps I should retire," she mumbled. "A headache." One shaky hand rose to press against her temple.

She might very well have had a headache for all she knew, but her entire body felt numb.

He wouldn't say anything—couldn't do anything—not in front of so many people. Her thoughts stuttered and lurched. She was safe. Blackwold was there, his hand under her arm, supporting her.

How could she have thought Blackwold was guilty? She should have confided in him, told him everything. But what else had there been for her to say?

Or was he in collusion with his uncle? No—he couldn't be—a small voice wailed.

"Henry, ring for Mary," Blackwold ordered, studying her face with a frown. "Do you feel faint?" A glimmer of humor shot through his brown eyes. "Perhaps you have no love for Mr. Haydn, either."

A hysterical laugh nearly choked her. She shook her head, her gaze locked on his neckcloth, not wanting to look at the vicar. A bit of black shifted at the edge of her vision. Carter stood and placed a hand against her back in apparent concern. She couldn't help jerking closer to Blackwold.

The appallingly cheerful music slowed and then stopped.

"What is wrong?" Lady Alice's high voice asked. "My poor Miss Cowles—are you unwell?"

"Headache," Hannah said again, closing her eyes.

Thankfully, Lady Alice pushed her way past the vicar and wrapped an arm around Hannah's waist. "My poor Miss Cowles. I know precisely what you are suffering. I have had the most dreadful headaches, myself. There is nothing for it but to lie down in a dark room." She shoved Blackwold away without a word of apology and led Hannah to the door. "Let me assist you—I know precisely what you require. My mama always insists on a glass of hot milk with butter when I am ill—she does not hold with the modern fashion of using laudanum at the slightest touch of pain."

When they reached the doorway, Gina rushed over to take Hannah's arm. "We will guide you—close your eyes if the light pains you, Hannah." Her chin tilted up, and she flashed a glance at Lady Alice when she used Hannah's name, as if to prove that she was a much better friend and therefore at liberty to use her Christian name.

The two girls pushed and pulled Hannah up the stairs to her room, their competition to comfort her only ending when Mary took firm control of Hannah and shut the bedroom door in the startled faces of Lady Alice and Gina.

Before she could protest, Hannah found herself tucked into bed with a warming pan at her feet and a glass of warm milk, butter, and rum on a small tray next to her bed. Mary fixed such a firm gaze on her that Hannah meekly picked up the glass and sipped the witch's brew. The first taste made her stomach roil in protest.

Mary pressed her lips together and crossed her arms.

Holding her breath, Hannah took several more swallows, each one growing a little easier. Finally, she set the glass back on the tray and slid down under the covers, pressing her feet against the towel-wrapped warming pan. The chill slowly began to leave her, along with the terrible numbness.

Mary picked up the tray. "Rest, Miss. No need to worry 'bout them below."

"I'm not worried about them," Hannah assured her sleepily.

"Very good, Miss." She closed the door softly behind her.

Hannah rolled over to face the windows. A soft gleam of moonlight threaded through a gap in the heavy drapes. She needed to think—to consider what Carter Hodges had said. She could have been wrong, could have leapt to the wrong conclusion. He could simply have meant that the waves had pounded the victims to death against the rocks, as had certainly happened to at least a few of them.

But what a strange word to use... *Bludgeon.*

And that look in his gray eyes—that flash of recognition. He knew that she knew, that she suspected him.

Or had she misread him completely? Warmth spread through her, the rum making it difficult to concentrate. She felt herself falling. For a moment, she resisted, but the pillows were so comfortable cradling her head and her nightgown felt so soft against her skin. She jerked once, blinking in the moonlight, and then gave in.

The morning was soon enough to consider what she now knew. For now, she could sleep...

<u>Chapter Nineteen</u>

The sound of paper rustling awoke her. Hannah glanced around her darkened room, confused by the sound. The thin shaft of moonlight shining through the narrow opening between the window's drapes barely provided sufficient light to see. She rolled over to face the door. A small, white square on the floor caught her attention.

A note? She propped herself up on one elbow. Sleep had deserted her—she felt wide awake. The fire had burned down to a few glowing coals in the fireplace. She padded over, picked up a spill from a small box sitting near the neatly stacked firewood, and lit it from a coal. Her bare feet already growing cold, she crept back and lit the candle on her bedside table.

Another glance revealed that it was indeed a small square of paper on her floor. The noise that had awakened her must have occurred when the note was shoved under her door. She looked at the clock on the mantle. Two-thirty in the morning. She picked up the note and unfolded it, holding it near the flickering candle.

Three—time for the truth. Meet me at the bottom of the garden path.

No signature. She frowned and then shook her head. Three in the morning was Blackwold's favored time for conversation, but why outside? Why didn't he just come to her room as he usually did?

Because his betrothed is in the room next to mine. Apparently, he did have some sense of discretion.

Mumbling very unpleasant comments about Blackwold, Hannah hurriedly threw on her warmest flannel petticoat and an old but serviceable wool traveling gown. Hardly an inspiring costume for a private rendezvous at the edge of the garden, but she wasn't feeling particularly inspired. She stifled a yawn as she grabbed a thick shawl.

The hallway was deserted when she gently opened her door. She waited a moment, listening, and then crept through the quiet house to the terrace door in the library.

As she unlocked it, she grimaced. It would be just her luck if some servant found the door unlocked and relocked it, leaving her outside with Blackwold all night.

That would be almost as difficult to explain as Lady Alice discovering him in Hannah's room at three in the morning.

Thick clouds obscured the moon and the stars, making the garden path appear dark, despite the lack of leaves on the low shrubs. Hannah shivered and drew her shawl more closely as she descended the terrace steps to the gravel path. The wind whipped around her, making her heavy skirts flap and twist around her limbs and tearing at her heavy braid which hung down her back.

Regretting her failure to put on a bonnet, she strode forward. There was no sign of Blackwold in the gardens proper, so she continued to the rough area between the gardens and the cliff. She smiled, thinking of Gina and the curate, bottoms in the air, examining the ground.

A cold drop of rain hit her nose. She wiped it off on her sleeve and cursed Blackwold. It seemed increasingly likely that he'd sent her out to get drenched by the coming storm while he'd stayed—warm and dry—inside, toasting his toes next to the fire and chuckling.

She was just about to turn back when something sharp pricked her back.

The silly wind must have whipped a rose branch against her. Now, she was going to have to waste time untangling her shawl from the vicious bush's thorns. Scowling, she caught up her shawl and half-turned.

Instead of a rose bush, she found herself staring at the muffled face of a man, tall and shadowed in the bulky darkness of his greatcoat. He held a sharp dagger in his left hand, its point aimed at her.

"Go on, Miss Cowles. No need to stop here."

When she didn't move, he made a short, stabbing motion with the fifteen-inch blade. It pricked through her shawl and her sleeve.

"What are you doing? Who are you?" she asked sharply as she moved to face him more fully.

"You know who I am—I saw it in your face. Now walk." He stabbed at her again with a sharp, jerking motion.

She instinctively stepped back, clutching her arms. The wind picked up, pulling fine hairs out of her braid and whipping them across her face. Inching back another step, she stared at him. Her heart pounded against her ribs, and her palms grew damp and icy.

Who—earlier? Her thoughts jumbled together, fear making it difficult to think. Then it clicked into place like a stiff door latch. Her dread coalesced into a cold, clear block of terror.

Carter Hodges.

"Mr. Hodges," she whispered. "Why—what do you want?"

"You represent a risk I am unprepared to accept. You saw me."

"No." She shook her head as he forced her to back up another step.

"Lying is a sin, Miss Cowles. I suggest you avoid such low behavior in your last few minutes."

"Last minutes?"

"Walk!"

"Where? Where do you want to go?" Another heavy drop of rain hit her on the forehead, cascading down over her right brow into her eye. She blinked furiously. "It is raining—I'm returning to the house."

"No, Miss Cowles. You are walking to the cliff."

"I will not." She straightened and crossed her arms over her shawl. "If you stab me, they will recognize the wound, even if you throw my body over the cliff. I will not go."

Her brief moment of defiance ended abruptly when he hit her savagely on the left shoulder with a cane—a weapon she hadn't seen him holding in his right hand.

Pain exploded in her arm. She stumbled and nearly went down on her knees. Her right hand flew to her shoulder. Shock and the freezing wind kept some of the agony at bay, but in the back of her mind, she knew it would grow unbearable soon.

She forced the thought, and her growing fear, aside.

"Now, Miss Cowles. Walk. Or I will beat you to death where you stand and drag you." He shrugged, holding the dagger in one hand and the cane in the other. "It matters not to me."

Staggering and cradling her left arm against her waist, she moved toward the cliff.

Think! There has to be a way to escape.

The rising storm howled in a burst of energy, tearing at her as if to force her away from the danger ahead. Her face stung under a sharp splattering of icy rain. Even the heavens seemed to rage and wail against them, trying to push them back to the safety of the house, but the vicar pressed on. He hit her again on the left side.

This time, she felt the pain clearly. A sob broke from her, and she stumbled, falling to her knees. Her entire arm and shoulder burned, throbbing with each heartbeat. Still, she couldn't give up, couldn't let him win. There had to be something she could do.

Once again, she staggered to her feet, looking around. They were closer, now. The edge was only twenty feet away. Crossing her right arm over her chest to protect her left side, she edged sideways.

"Why now? Why at three in the morning?" She had to yell to be heard over the increasing tumult of the storm.

Carter's mouth twisted into a smile. "Three is the most honest time of the day. Did Blackwold not tell you? It is well known. Amongst the Hodges, at least. We are all poor sleepers, and three has always been the time for confidences. The truth." He shrugged, his greatcoat flapping around his legs. "It seemed appropriate. And I knew you would come if you thought *he'd* summoned you."

She shook her head.

"I felt sure he would have enlightened you."

"Just what are you suggesting?" She tried to sound insulted instead of simply terrified. If she could maneuver him closer to the cliff, perhaps... She took another step to his left, courting the dagger rather than the brutal cane.

"Exactly what you believe." His mechanical voice was clear above the wind. He sounded bored.

What she thought, any questions she had, were unimportant to him. Their conversation, brief as it was, was finished. She flinched further to his left.

The vicar raised his cane again, a monstrous black figure against the swirling gray clouds above.

Then something dark barreled out of the night. It slammed into the vicar. His dagger flew one way and his cane the other as he landed on the ground. Hannah dashed around the writhing figures and picked up the dagger in her good hand.

Low grunting revealed the presence of another man. The two rolled through the mud, locked together. Glancing around, Hannah ran to the cane—it had more reach than the dagger—she couldn't let Carter get it. But her left arm was useless, and she couldn't hold both the dagger and the stick. Without thinking, she threw the dagger over the edge of the cliff and picked up the cane.

If Carter managed to free himself... She was not going to let him force her—or anyone else—over the cliff.

The rain was pouring down in heavy sheets, and she blinked, trying to clear the water out of her eyes.

First one man and then the other got to his feet. They faced each other, hunched like two animals preparing to fight.

"Stop!" she yelled. "There is no need..."

One of them—Carter—she recognized his white face—glanced at her and then back at his opponent. He seemed to straighten. Standing at the edge of the cliff, he appeared immensely tall against the chiaroscuro background of the storm clouds. His hat was gone, and he raised his face to the rain.

Washing his sins away. The thought rushed through Hannah as she impulsively took a step forward. *Don't...*

Then he was gone.

"No!" she screamed, horrified. Burning tears mingled with the cold rain sluicing down her cheeks.

"He chose his own way. As usual." Blackwold's deep voice carried over the sounds of the storm. "Are you injured?" He moved closer to her, but didn't touch her.

The rain made it difficult to see him clearly, but she had the notion that his cravat was missing, his waistcoat undone, and his jacket was rumpled and clotted with mud.

She'd never seen anyone so dear to her in her life. Laughter—partly hysterical, partly relief, and mostly just the sheer joy of being alive and in love—bubbled out of her.

"Are you well?" he asked, sounding very unsure.

"Yes—no. I'm just so glad to see you." The words gushed out of her.

When he moved to put an arm around her, she backed away.

"My arm—" she stammered.

"Is it broken?" He stopped a foot away, his arms bent as if he wanted to hold her but was afraid of breaking her into tiny pieces.

"Yes—I don't know—perhaps." Now that she had the luxury of experiencing every little ache and pain, she found it hurt even to talk. Every breath, every small movement, sent another hot stab of agony through her shoulder and radiating down her arm.

He moved around to her right side, slipped a gentle arm around her waist, and urged her toward the house.

"Carter—"

"Do you truly want to discuss him now?" Blackwold asked.

"It is better than thinking about my arm."

Blackwold chuckled and then sobered. "Sorry—didn't mean to laugh. You are in pain."

"I'd rather laugh than cry," Hannah remarked, doing her best not to moan, be sick, or fall to her knees with hysterical sobs.

"Precisely." He held the door for her and ushered her inside. "Can you make it to your room?"

She gritted her teeth. "It's my arm, not my lower limbs."

"Oh? I didn't know ladies *had* lower limbs."

A laugh escaped her, followed closely by a moan. "Stop it," she gasped. "You're just tormenting me for your own foul purposes."

"Fowl?" He glanced around. "Oh, you must have heard the gardener's rooster. Crowing a bit early—the storm must have roused him. Is that what awakened you?"

She tied her shawl to support her left arm and clutched the banister with her good hand. "Go away."

"Mary will attend you shortly." He leaned over the handrail, caught her chin in one hand, and pressed a kiss on her lips. "Followed by Dr. Burland."

Despite the unexpected pleasure of his kiss, she groaned again and shook her head, hoping he wouldn't notice her flushed cheeks.

"Be of good cheer. Even though you lack a fever, I'm sure he'll be happy to bleed you. Just ask him."

She sighed and tried not to roll her eyes.

He grinned and stood back. "And I will check on our supply of linen bandages." One of his brows flew up. "You are awfully prone to accidents, you know. Are all Americans so careless?"

Caught between a fresh burst of laughter, agony, and complete aggravation, Hannah gripped the banister and moved as gently as she could to avoid jarring her aching arm. "I refuse to respond to that ridiculous question," she said through gritted teeth.

"Is that not a response?"

"Go away! Fetch the doctor. I can only hope he manages to drain every last drop of my blood this time, so you will all leave me in peace."

"Hope does seem to spring eternal," he called before slipping away into the shadows.

Chapter Twenty

The physician didn't bleed her after all, and he was huffily disappointed by that and the fact that her arm and shoulder weren't actually broken, just badly bruised. And perhaps a small fracture, though he couldn't be sure. The thought created a small, tight smile on his serious face. By the time he stopped poking and prodding Hannah, she was ready to pick up the cane she'd inadvertently carried to her room caught in her shawl and beat him over the head with it. Just to give him an idea of what her shoulder felt like.

Unlike Lady Northrop, Dr. Burland had no scruples about the liberal use of laudanum. He ensured his patient had a generous swallow of the milky liquid, mixed into a glass of water, before he left.

Feeling overly warm, the ache receded, and Hannah slept.

When she awoke, muzzy-headed and slightly sick to her stomach, Gina was sitting next to her bed, reading a book. Hannah blinked, and the light from her window dimmed and brightened. Lady Alice moved into view, followed by Mary, who was frowning at the two young women.

"I warned you girls to leave her in peace!" Mary complained. She spread her arms and walked toward Lady Alice as if to shoo her out of the room.

"But I want to talk to her!" Gina wailed, closing her book. She glanced at Hannah and back at Mary, her chin rising and lower lip thrust out defiantly. "And she's already awake, so there is no point in us leaving, now." She held up a hand. "You cannot blame us—you are most likely the one who awakened her."

"How are you feeling, Miss Cowles?" Lady Alice asked shyly from the foot of the bed.

Terrible. Hannah forced a smile, but didn't dare move. Her arm and shoulder did not hurt at the moment as they were still warm and numb with sleep. However, she had the feeling that once she fully woke up and moved, the pain would return two-fold.

"Please, call me Hannah," she said to Lady Alice. She looked at the bedside table. No tea or water. Her mouth felt sticky, with an unpleasant taste in it.

Lady Alice smiled with pleasure.

"Tea—that'll be what you need." Mary slipped past the girls and left, her determined footsteps clacking down the hallway.

"What happened to you?" Gina asked, leaning over the edge of the bed.

Hannah opened her mouth and then shut it again. She could hardly tell the girl that her uncle had tried to murder her. Her eyes glanced around the room before she focused on Gina. "Have you spoken to Lord Blackwold?"

"Oh, yes!" Gina clasped her hands together. Her eyes glittered with excitement, and then the glow suddenly vanished like a candle blown out. "Poor Uncle Carter. You did your best to save him, though." She grasped Hannah's good wrist and gave it a squeeze. "You cannot blame yourself—you were so brave—you did everything you could, I'm sure."

So Blackwold had not told them everything.

Hannah sighed and shifted in bed. She immediately regretted the small movement. A bolt of pain shot through her arm. She gritted her teeth and closed her eyes, trying not to be ill.

"It is so tragic," Lady Alice said. "But how did you happen to see the vicar out on the lawn?"

"The curtains were slightly open—I got up to close them when the storm started." Hannah stared at the open drapes, trying to order her thoughts and guess what tale Blackwold might have told to explain what had happened. "I saw him in the gardens and was worried for his safety."

"Why did you not ring for Mary?" Gina asked. Her gaze was a trifle too sharply inquisitive for comfort.

"I did not think about it. With the storm coming—I thought Mr. Hodges was in danger—I wanted to warn him."

"But why was he out there?" Lady Alice studied her, her hands clasped around one of the bed poles. She leaned forward, the sunlight gilding her fair hair and turning her pale blue morning gown white where the beam played over the sleeves and shoulders.

Lies, partial truths, and the complete truth whirled through her. "I truly don't know. I saw him in the garden and went to warn him. By the time I reached him, the gale winds had pushed him toward the cliff. There was nothing I could do—I am truly sorry, Georgina." She used Gina's formal name because, in some strange sense, she did feel responsible for the death of her uncle.

Gina didn't know what her uncle had been doing to increase his wealth. The thought made her feel ill. The money Mr. Hodges had obtained from the wreckage of the *Orion* had probably been sufficient to allow him the luxury of hiring his new curate, Mr. Furlong, for one thing.

Well, Gina definitely didn't need to know *that*.

Gina sniffed and touched a flimsy, lace-edge handkerchief to her eyes. Her small nose was crimson, and her eyes were rimmed with red, and Hannah recognized the signs proving that Gina had been crying before she came to Hannah's room.

She couldn't move her bruised arm, so she shifted her right wrist enough to catch Gina's hand and give it a squeeze. "I truly am sorry."

"Uncle Carter was always k-kind to me," Gina said, her voice shaking and catching on her words. "I could not believe it when we awoke to the news that he had fallen from the cliff. Why was he there?"

"I don't know, Gina. I doubt we shall ever know." She gave the girl's hand another warm squeeze. "Perhaps you ought to see how your grandmother is—this cannot be easy for her, particularly when she's been so ill."

Gina sniffed and rose to her feet. "She was asleep the last time I went to her room. It grieves me so—I can hardly face her." A sob broke through her voice, and she covered her face with her hands before turning and dashing through the door.

Hannah let out another sigh before a movement caught her attention. Lady Alice remained standing at the foot of Hannah's bed.

"How terrible—I hope it does not prevent Georgina from joining us in London. A woman cannot put off her Season too long—each year makes such a difference. One loses her bloom and freshness so quickly, as I'm sure you have realized."

Hannah gave her a sharp glance, but there was no malice in Lady Alice's face. The girl simply had an exceedingly unfortunate way of phrasing her sentiments.

"Perhaps I should go, as well. You will need your rest." Lady Alice took a step toward the door.

"Wait—I have wanted to speak to you." Hannah raised her right hand and gestured to the chair next to her bed. "Are you completely happy with your betrothal?"

"Happy?" Confusion wrinkled her brow. She raised her left hand and chewed on the edge of her index finger before she realized what she was doing, flushed, and lowered her hand to her lap. "It is an excellent match."

"But don't you wish to marry for love? Or at least, affection?"

"Of course." Lady Alice smiled.

"But you don't love Lord Blackwold, do you?"

She shook her head and giggled uncomfortably. Her gaze refused to meet Hannah's and drifted over to stare at the window. "No, of course not. He is so, well, *rumpled.* How could anyone admire that?"

"Then why marry him?"

"He's a marquess!" Lady Alice flashed a wide-eyed, startled glance at Hannah.

Hannah studied her. "Is a title so important that you'd marry someone you don't even care for, when there is someone nearby you do admire? And who admires you?"

"Admires me?" Her delicate hand flew to press against her heart. Her blue eyes glowed above flushed cheeks.

"Yes—Mr. Henry Hodges. Surely, you've noticed—a blind woman would have noticed. And he admitted it to me."

"Henry? Did he truly tell you that he admired me?" She half-rose off the seat and clasped both hands together. Her eyes blazed as she looked at Hannah.

"Yes, he did." Hannah relaxed and took a deep breath. "I wanted to ensure you knew."

All of a sudden, Lady Alice plunked down on the chair. The wooden legs screeched against the floorboards, but the girl didn't notice. The color in her cheeks faded to gray, and her gaze hardened. "Nonetheless, my mother will insist. He is a marquess, after all."

"Henry is the cousin of a marquess—surely that counts for something."

"It is not a title. He is Mr. Hodges."

"And you shall still be Lady Alice, one way or the other. So, I can't see that it matters so much."

"It does. It matters a great deal." Lady Alice sighed and rose to her feet. "I should allow you to rest. I am so sorry you were injured." She nodded and slipped out of Hannah's bedroom before Hannah could reply.

Why did so many people refuse to take the road that might lead to happiness? She'd only wanted to help Lady Alice, and spare her a loveless marriage to a man for whom she obviously cherished few—if any—tender feelings.

And Blackwold... What would his life be like, married to a woman who would forever be trying to *manage* him and make him into something he was not? Who didn't even understand his sense of humor?

Hannah was well aware that she had no hope in that direction—she was not a fool, even if she'd fallen foolishly in love with the wrong man. But her decision to return to

Boston now felt as firm as if she'd already purchased the ticket. That decision left her with the sense that she needed to do something to set things right at Blackrock before she left. There had been too many tragedies already.

Lady Alice should marry Henry Hodges, not Lord Blackwold.

Blackwold would find some other lady in London. Hopefully, one who laughed at his terrible jokes and would find the lock of shaggy hair hanging over his eyes charming.

And Gina should marry Mr. Furlong. It was rare to find someone who shared the same interests—too rare to toss away. She remembered her parents pouring over maps, sharing their deep love of travel...

Before Hannah could decide on a strategy, Mary returned with tea and a light breakfast. Fragrant buns, still steaming under a linen napkin, filled the room with the scent of warm, yeasty bread, and pots of marmalade and fresh butter framed a gilt-edged china plate. Hannah's stomach burbled with emptiness.

Despite Mary's attempts to keep her in bed, Hannah convinced her to help her dress, and left her room in search of Henry Hodges. The longcase clock in the hallway chimed a single mellow tone as she went downstairs and wandered into the library.

"Miss Cowles! Should you be downstairs?" Henry leapt to his feet, scattering the sheets of a newspaper over the floor and the small table next to his chair.

"I am quite well—just a little bruised," she said, gliding across the floor as smoothly as possible. When she took firm footsteps, she had to grit her teeth against the jarring motion that made her bruises flare to life.

"Please—sit down." He gestured to a settee near his chair. Glancing down, he hastily bent and began collecting the printed sheets. He was wearing thin cotton gloves to protect his fingers from the ink, and he couldn't prevent himself from fussily organizing the papers into the correct order. Finally, he folded the newspaper along the original lines and placed it squarely on the center of the table at his elbow.

"Mr. Hodges, I have something I wish to discuss with you." Hannah cleared her throat and rested her right forearm over her left in her lap. "I have received some bad news."

"Not the letter my uncle brought from the bank, I hope. We have all been concerned about the contents of that note." As he studied her, his brows furrowed, and he frowned. "Do you have the letter with you? Perhaps I can be of service to you."

"Not at the moment. No." She took a deep breath. "It appears I am no longer the heiress I was originally. The largest part of my fortune has been lost—the courier absconded with it before it could be deposited in the Bank of England."

"My dear Miss Cowles!" Henry leaned forward and tried to take her good hand, but she pulled it away with a twisted smile.

"I thought you should know—and we must inform the dowager, as well. I do not think that the mere possibility of a title, particularly not one of baron, can make up for such a loss."

"No," Henry murmured thoughtfully, sitting back in his chair. "However, there may be income from the estate…"

"Perhaps. However, if they are in ruins, it may take a great deal of capital to set them to rights before any income can be derived from them. Assuming that it is even possible to restore the title and estates to my family—my husband, to be more precise." She leaned toward him. "The risks are great for so small a reward, particularly when one's affections are engaged elsewhere."

Henry blinked. "Elsewhere? I assure you, Miss Cowles, that I am very fond of you."

"I will not mince words. There is someone you are a great deal fonder of, if you would only thrust the ridiculous matter of titles aside. Lady Alice admires you greatly, and

I believe you harbor a great deal of affection for her. It would be a good match for both of you, if you would only consider it."

A flash in Henry's gray eyes told her that not only had he considered it, he was in favor of it. But just as quickly as the light appeared in his eyes, it died. He shook his head. "Blackwold..."

"Yes?" Blackwold strolled into the library, looking as cheerfully disheveled as ever. His neckcloth was completely missing today, his waistcoat hung open, and his linen shirt was crumpled. His brown jacket looked as if he'd slept in it. The fresh scents of sea air and bay from his shaving soap whirled into the room around him, and Hannah couldn't help but smile.

A warm rush of emotion filled her, tightening her throat. "Mr. Hodges was advising me," she said, smoothing her gown over her lap. "I received word that my inheritance has been lost. I have decided to return to Boston to discover what can be salvaged." She flushed and glanced first at Blackwold and then at Henry. "Unfortunately—and embarrassingly—I find I will have to write my lawyer to request that he purchase a ticket for me. I have no account here on which to draw." Though she could, if necessary, sell her jewels as a last resort. A terrible last resort. Once sold, they—and the memories they carried of her mother wearing the glittering stones—would be gone forever.

"Henry—get out," Blackwold said, flopping into a wing chair next to his cousin. He hooked one knee over the arm and began swinging his foot.

"I beg your pardon!" Henry stood. His glance alternated between Hannah and Blackwold.

"Get out—Lady Alice is in the garden, no doubt weeping decorously and much more in need of your advice than Miss Cowles." He studied his fingernails and bit off a hangnail on his right hand. "Had a bit of a shock." Flashing a grin at his cousin, Blackwold jerked his head back to fling the hair out of his eyes. "Seems our lawyers couldn't come to terms on the marriage contract." He sighed. "Well, you can't say we didn't try."

"You—you are not betrothed?" Pale, Henry's hand clenched and unclenched at his sides. He licked his lower lip.

"No. We are not. Most definitely not."

"I beg your pardon." He jerked a bow in Hannah's direction before smoothing his hair with a shaky hand. "Dreadful news. Shock. In the garden, you say?"

"Garden. Go." Blackwold pointed to the door. "Hie thee hence, varlet."

With shaky legs, Henry surged toward the terrace door, randomly bumping into furniture and shoving it out of his way before he managed to reach the French doors and stumble through them.

"What about Gina?" she asked, trying to control the elation fizzing through her, making it nearly impossible to remain seated. Her toes tapped the carpet in front of her chair.

"What about her?"

"You cannot send her to London and callously force her into marriage with some titled nincompoop. She and Mr. Furlong—"

"She shall have her Mr. Furlong, if she wants the beanpole. Contrary to any tales of woe she may have whispered into your ear, her father is ridiculously indulgent. If she wishes to marry Miles Furlong, then marry Miles Furlong she shall. Though why she should be attracted to a bespectacled beanpole is past understanding." He scratched his neck below one ear. "The Hodges are not all cold-hearted murderers."

"Well," Hannah said. Initially relieved that Gina wouldn't be forced into a loveless marriage, she soon shifted uncomfortably and flushed. She owed him an apology—she had suspected him of terrible deeds—and she couldn't help but believe that she was in some way responsible for the death of his uncle. "I am so sorry."

"You wish more Hodges were cold-hearted murderers? What a bloodthirsty little minx you are." He rubbed his chin and yawned. "Well, I can't say as I've ever wished to murder anyone, but if it will make you happy... Did you have someone particular in mind, or just the first stranger who knocks on the door?"

"No!" A laugh caught in her throat. "Please stop it—I'm trying to be serious."

"Well, I've always considered murder to be a quite serious business."

"I was only offering you sympathy—"

"Don't. No need to remind me of Lady Alice. The thought of being managed fills me with horror."

"What?" She stifled a giggle and tried to maintain a serious expression. "I meant, I'm trying to offer you sympathy over your uncle."

"Why?" He tilted his head and studied her with gleaming, amused eyes.

"Well—I mean—he was your uncle."

"Unfortunately."

As he studied her, she felt a flush heating her cheeks. "Last night—how did you happen—that is—thank you... Oh, you know what I am trying to say." She threw her good hand up in a gesture of helplessness. So many conflicting emotions and questions plagued her that she hardly knew where to begin.

"You left that blasted note behind, you know. On your bed. Found it when I came to continue our discussion." He grinned at her, his foot swinging more rapidly.

"Why *did* you come to my room to chat? Your betrothed was right next door—how could you?"

His brows rose. "My betrothed? She never was my betrothed. Wanted to be—thought she might do—but... No. And you should have realized, Miss Cowles, that I have been bedeviled with concerns for you and your safety. Knew wreckers were working the coast, and someone was working with them. Why the devil didn't you confide in me?"

"I didn't know! I told you, all I saw was that ridiculous ring you all wear. How was I to know which one of you was wearing it?"

"The eyes—"

"The eyes!" She snorted. "No one could see the difference between little chips of diamonds and topaz! During a storm, no less!"

"His voice is unmistakable."

"Yes, it is," she replied sharply. "Under normal circumstances. When one isn't being assaulted by wind and waves."

He shrugged and chuckled. He sobered almost immediately, though, and glanced at the hallway door. "The dowager is taking it badly, however. I must ask you, Miss Cowles—"

"Hannah, please."

"Hannah, please." His mouth twisted into a shy grin. "I dislike begging—even in dogs—but might you maintain your exquisitely perceptive silence concerning my uncle's activities? My grandmother believes you were injured trying to save my uncle's life. The tale is that he must have seen something that drew him to the cliff—a ship in distress, perhaps—and the gale caught him. An unfortunate accident."

"I will do so, never fear. But what shall you say when she questions why he was in the garden at night? Surely he can't see the ocean from the vicarage?"

"No." He laughed. "But that is not difficult. My uncle provided the excuse, himself. He claimed a ferocious dislike of superstition. Of late, he'd been trying to disprove the tales of a Lady of the Mist. I suspect his diligence in rooting out the superstition was actually to provide him with an excellent way to explain his other, less savory activities if he should be seen around the cliffs at night." He shrugged. "Regardless, it is a well-known excuse and should serve us well enough."

"I wish..." She pressed her lips together and gave her head a shake. "Why did he have to jump?"

"He knew he would have been arrested and questioned." A shadow passed over Blackwold's face. He stared, unseeing, past Hannah's shoulder. "He must have known I was working with Farley, the local Customs Officer—and an idiot if ever there was one—to put an end to Carter's activities. I would have liked to question him, though, to discover who else was involved." He shrugged and let out a long breath. "I did know they used the church's crypt to store some goods. I had hoped the wreckers did so without Carter's knowledge."

"But after I saw that ring, you knew it had to be one of you."

"Yes." His mouth twisted. "And I knew I was not involved."

"I see, and I'm sorry." She suddenly felt empty, bereft of purpose and alone. She shifted on the settee uncomfortably and cradled her injured arm again. She raised her chin and looked at Blackwold. "As I was explaining to Henry, I would like to return to Boston—to determine the extent of my losses."

"I can't say that I'm impressed with your lawyer's competence thus far, but my man can ensure he gives us an accounting. I shouldn't worry about it."

"Well, you may not be worried about it, but I am! I can hardly stay here as a guest of your grandmother's for the rest of my life! Particularly after... Well, all things considered."

"Why not? You haven't even reached the month mark, and several of Grandmother's acquaintances have managed to squeeze out twice that time. One lady managed an entire year."

"I have no wish to take advantage of her! Even you admitted that I was not the imposter you feared I was, so it should not be too difficult to believe that I have behaved in good conscience the entire time I have been here!" She stood up and instantly regretted it. All the blood seemed to flow out of her head. She swayed and pressed cold fingertips to her temple, waiting for the room to stop spinning.

Blackwold got to his feet as well and strode over to her, steadying her with one firm hand on her shoulder. Warmth spread through her at his touch, and she felt the prick of tears.

How could she go? She loved him so much that she could barely keep from catching his arm and drawing him close enough to bury her face into his coat. She wanted to breathe in his mingled fragrance of salt air, bay soap, and the underlying rich scent of his sun-warmed skin.

Trying to find something from which to build a wall, something strong enough to shield her heart, she fixed her gaze on his wrinkled shirt. No matter what he said, surely he'd felt something for Lady Alice, or he wouldn't have been so complaisant about their near betrothal.

He would never admire someone like her—a young, sweet girl.

And she couldn't forget that he'd been the one who disputed her identity so vociferously. He hadn't trusted her then, and she saw no reason for him to harbor any affection for her now, despite his teasing kisses.

In the end, she would have to return to Boston sooner or later. So, in silent desperation, she thought again of Lady Alice. She was a flimsy barricade, to be sure, but she was all Hannah had.

And she was fairly sure that the dowager and Lady Northrop would have something to say about the sudden change in the couple's understanding.

"But what about Lady Alice?" Hannah asked, her voice squeaking. Her feet danced nervously as she tried to think—to remain calm and disinterested.

"Lady Alice? Again?" He let out a long, exaggerated sigh. "Perhaps she can obtain music lessons when she goes to London. Otherwise, I don't have much hope for her. Henry has quite a good ear for music."

"I wasn't talking about the pianoforte. That is not at all what I meant, and you know it." She laughed and couldn't help adding, "You are not tone deaf, either. Are you?"

"Actually, I am," he replied apologetically. He shifted her closer, staring down at her tenderly as he brushed a strand of hair away from her cheek. "So, the fact that Lady Alice is somewhat less than competent at the keyboard doesn't matter to me in the least. But my grandmother is a brilliant musician—or was before her hands were crippled with arthritis—and Henry is quite musical. So, I heroically threw myself into the breach last night. It was only my admission of that inexcusable weakness that forestalled any need for Grandmother to comment upon that wretched girl's performance. Or for Henry to notice the fissure in Lady Alice's perfection. Noble of me, was it not?" he asked, pretending solemn modesty, despite the wicked gleam in his brown eyes.

Snorting with laughter, Hannah tried to maintain a calm and serious demeanor, but failed miserably. "Please stop making me laugh—it's very cruel and unsuitable of you."

"But I love your laugh—it fills our darkest rooms with sunshine. And it is the one thing I can count on to be honest and pure. So, I can not, and will not, promise not to make you laugh. I will do so in as many circumstances, and as often, as possible."

She smothered a giggle. "Well, I wish you luck for I am returning to Boston—"

"You are *not* returning, my dear girl. You are my Miss Cowles, *lately* of Boston, and that closes the matter."

"I can't stay here," she murmured, despite the touch of Blackwold's lips upon her own. "Lady Alice—"

"Will you forget Lady Alice?"

Her fragile wall crumbled. Her right hand touched one of the wrinkles in his shirt, smoothing it as she shook her head.

"Well, that is unfortunate as you can't leave." He gently deepened the kiss, angling her to avoid crushing her injured arm.

"I—"

"Miss Cowles—Hannah—for once in your life, consider someone else's sentiments." Smiling, he pressed his lips to her forehead.

"I have done nothing else!"

He raised his brows as he grinned at her. "I hadn't noticed any particular care for my feelings."

"Your feelings?"

"My heart has been in your careless hands since my grandmother fished you out of the ocean."

"Your *heart?!* Fished me *out?!*" Laughter mingled with snorts of aggravation as the breath caught in her throat. A warm feeling rushed through her. "What of my feelings?"

"What of them?"

"This is not a laughing matter." She broke off in a helpless fit of giggles before she gasped and clutched her injured arm. "Oh, please, don't make me laugh—it hurts."

He sobered immediately and pressed a tender kiss to her cheek. "Then accept my apologies and my love—I would never hurt you. I did my best to ensure your safety." A look of anger hardened his face, and the hand he'd slipped behind her head tightened for a moment. "I nearly failed you—"

"But you did not."

"You were injured."

"My arm isn't even broken—I believe Dr. Burland was very disappointed by that. And I couldn't even persuade him to bleed me. All-in-all, a very unsatisfactory ending for a heroine."

"I do love you, Hannah," he said, his gaze catching hers.

"Well, that's fortunate, because I love you, as well. Even when you make me laugh when you know it hurts."

"I'm a beast."

"Yes, you are. A great big brown bear of a beast."

"Then will the beauty tame the bear?" His gaze drifted to her mouth.

She smiled, her world expanding as wide as the sunlit sky over the ocean. "Not tame—love." She reached up and brushed the shaggy brown lock of hair out of his eyes, and laughed for the sheer joy of it. His hair felt so soft, so warm as the strands threaded between her fingers. "Just don't make me laugh—at least for an hour or so. *Please.*"

In answer, he kissed her, making it impossible for her to think of laughing, or crying, or ever returning to Boston again.

THE END

Your Opinion Matters: Thank you for reading my book. Your opinion is important to other readers, as well as to me. Readers use reviews to find new books to read, and authors are always desperate to obtain reviews because 4 and 5 star reviews are required to advertise and promote our books. I know that the time and effort required to write a review can make the task daunting, but even a few words are helpful. So, if you have time to write a review on Amazon, I would really appreciate it.

Thank you again for taking the time to read my book. I sincerely hope you enjoyed it.

Other Titles by Amy Corwin

The Archer Family Regency Romance Series

The **Archer Family series** are traditional Regency romances spiced with a mystery.

While these books do not need to be read in order, the list below presents them in the series order.

The Necklace (Prequel to the series)
The Unwanted Heiress
A Lady in Hiding
The Earl's Masquerade
A Stolen Rose
En Garde, My Love
Love Across the Pond

Regency Romantic Mysteries

Regency Romantic Mysteries are sweet Regency romances with a touch of mystery. While they are stand-alone novels, they all take place in the late Regency/early Victorian period and have a similar "feel" to them.

All She Loves

Second Sons Inquiry Agency Regency Mystery Series

The **Second Sons Inquiry Agency series** are traditional historical mysteries set in the Regency period in England. The books all feature the Second Sons Inquiry Agency.

While these books do not need to be read in order, the list below presents them in a series order.

The Vital Principle
A Rose Before Dying
The Dead Man's View
The Illusion of Desire

Honeymoon with Death

A Second Chance Paranormal Romances

The **Second Chance Paranormal Romances** are paranormal tales spiced with mystery, danger and an "Urban Fantasy" feel. They do not have to be read in any particular order as each book stands alone.

Her Vampire Bodyguard
A Fall of Silver

Paranormal Suspense

Month of Judgment

Mysteries

A new series of contemporary, cozy mysteries is underway, set in fictitious towns near the Outer Banks of North Carolina.

Whacked!
Deadly Inheritance

About the Author

Amy Corwin is a charter member of the Romance Writers of America and recently joined Mystery Writers of America. She writes historical and cozy mysteries with a touch of romance, as well as paranormal romances. To be truthful, most of her books include a bit of murder and mayhem since she discovered that killing off at least one character is a highly effective way to make the remaining ones toe the plot line.

Her books include the historical mysteries, Regency romances, paranormal romances and mysteries.

Join her and discover that every good mystery has a touch of romance.

Connect with Me Online

Website: http://www.amycorwin.com

Twitter: http://twitter.com/amycorwin

Facebook: http://www.facebook.com/AmyCorwinAuthor

Blog: http://amycorwin.blogspot.com

Amy Corwin

www.ingramcontent.com/pod-product-compliance
Lightning Source LLC
Chambersburg PA
CBHW031954170626
46807CB00006B/2477